T0037243

SUIZA

Bénédicte Belpois

SUIZA

*Translated from the French
by Alison Anderson*

Europa
editions

Europa Editions
1 Penn Plaza, Suite 6282
New York, N.Y. 10019
www.europaeditions.com
info@europaeditions.com

This book is a work of fiction. Any references to historical events,
real people, or real locales are used fictitiously.

Copyright © Editions Gallimard, Paris, 2019
First publication 2021 by Europa Editions

Translation by Alison Anderson
Original title: *Suiza*
Translation copyright © 2021 by Europa Editions

All rights reserved, including the right of reproduction
in whole or in part in any form.

Library of Congress Cataloging in Publication Data is available
ISBN 978-1-60945-707-5

Belpois, Bénédicte
Suiza

Book design by Emanuele Ragnisco
www.mekkanografici.com

Cover illustration by Ginevra Rapisardi

Prepress by Grafica Punto Print – Rome

Printed in Italy

For Élisabeth, Adélaïde, and Éléonore

"Now they have big, calm bodies,
hearts as simple as poppies."
—JEAN GIONO

SUIZA

P eople around here are bound to say anything they want about me, given what happened. Anything. That it was in my genes, the violence and boredom, that I really did take after my father and it was sure to happen anyway. They'll tell my life story, even to people who haven't asked a thing, who are just passing through, who are in the village to see someone they know, or to visit the region. But no one really knows the story, apart from Ramón. Agustina, too, come to think of it, but she couldn't be completely objective, I was like a son to her. It's mainly Ramón who'd have the right to tell it, because he practically lived with us.

He was the first one to find out that I was sick. I mean seriously ill, a really nasty disease. Yes, that's how it all started, the whole business. With a hell of a disgusting sickness.

It crept up on me, too, because I didn't realize right away. In the beginning, I was just hacking and spitting, I had a fever, I thought it was just the flu. I didn't even stop smoking. Don Confreixo loaded me with antibiotics, but it didn't go away. I felt awful. After a week, he sent me to the emergency room in Lugo, and there they threw the whole kit and caboodle at me. Scanned my lungs, then my whole body; doctors waltzing in and out to argue at the foot of my bed about what to do next, more tests and the diagnosis, while I was getting restless thinking about all the work I had left to do: haymaking was due to start in a few days, and one of my best tractors had broken down, not to mention the hygiene inspection, which wasn't looking good: there were still a few cases of bluetongue in Terra Chá that were blocking our exports. I finally managed to get out of there, without their approval, by asking them to transfer my file to my doctor once they'd finally agreed on the diagnosis and what to do next. But I could tell it wasn't looking good.

The very next day, Don Confreixo called me first thing after milking.

"Tomás? Are you back? You have to come by this morning, the hospital called, I have your results."

"I can't, Doctor. I've got an inspection for the herds. And I have to go to Orense about a tractor. I'm already behind."

"It's not a request, Tomás, you have to come in immediately. Please."

Ramón had just arrived, I was running toward the tractor, so I said, "Yeah, okay, sure," to get rid of him. I was just annoyed because I knew it would take up a morning's work.

When I was there in front of him, he put on his real doctor glasses and opened his mouth, then closed it again without saying anything, after taking a deep breath. He did this toad thing a few more times, it was pissing me off, so I said, fast as I could:

"Is it serious?"

"Yes."

"Cancer?"

"Yes," he answered, the bastard.

Straight out. He was having trouble swallowing and he looked at me as if he were some blind lemur, and it didn't take me long to figure out that if I was expecting him to butter me up and make me feel better I'd have to look elsewhere.

"How long have I got?"

I blurted it out without really thinking, because that's what they always say in the movies after they're told something like this. With an anxious face. The movie's in black and white, the hero tenses his jaw and whispers something out of the Bible in what sounds like his second-to-last breath.

"Tomás, hey, aren't you jumping the gun? We're here to talk about recovery, not how long you have to live."

Ah, he can squeeze out some positivity after all, the murderer.

I was looking at my hands, my big peasant mitts, I was thinking my nails still looked pretty clean in spite of everything, and I was wondering whether I'd have time for a swig of Rioja before going back to work.

Then came the protocol, and the appointments, the ones I'd have to go to, Don Confreixo was taking care of everything, but he wouldn't look me in the eye. He fiddled with my file, clearing his throat at regular intervals, and called his colleagues to get me an appointment pronto with some big-shot lung specialist.

I met Ramón at the bar.

"I have pleurisy. I'll probably have to go back to the hospital for a few days, for antibiotics, and more x-rays, maybe even an operation. Ask Alberto if he can come give you a hand while I'm in Lugo."

The farm was easy enough, old Ramón knew as well as I did what to do. The hardest part was packing my suitcase: I didn't even have any pajamas. I sleep naked. Or with all my clothes on, when I'm too drunk.

I had time for the Rioja. I even drank three, while the old man gave me the lowdown on the fields.

That's how it began, honestly. I'll try to tell the rest of it simply. Because I'm a pretty basic sort of guy, I'm not the psychopath they say I am. I did the best I could, but this thing hit me in the face, and I don't see how I could have acted differently.

I was almost glad to go to the hospital in the end.

The pajamas weren't a problem, I probably wasn't the only one. I put on the face of the twelve-year-old kid who doesn't have a nice mommy to put pajamas in his summer-camp suitcase, and the nurses' aides felt sorry for me and gave me this huge nightshirt, open in the back. My neighbor in the ward could see my ass whenever I got up to piss, even though I tried to keep the two sides together with my left hand. But since I was pushing the IV with my right hand at the same time, and I've always been about as agile as a dragster, I ended up showing him my butt cheeks every time, if I didn't want to bump into the bed, the door, the chair, and all the things they put there on purpose to piss me the fuck off and remind me that I was too tall, too fat, and too stupid.

I felt like telling the men in the white coats, go ahead, operate. Take out everything you possibly can: lungs, liver, spleen, heart. I don't want anything more to do with this rotten flesh, where some revolting thing is growing against my will. The doctors weren't all on the same page, it took them two days to decide that yes, they would cut into my ribs to go after the piece of shit devouring my lung.

Even after the operation, I think I was fine. It didn't hurt, I had my regular fix, in addition to the morphine pump that distilled a comatose bliss into my veins. They took care of me, no doubt about that. The nurses were kind, but they were fat and ugly: not a single one of them raised the bar, nothing to go on even for a little handjob. They weren't wearing garters or provocative necklines like in porn magazines, they had to run around all day and only came to flip me over like a pancake and wash my back with something that stank like a high-end eau de cologne. They got a kick out of washing my back, I never found out why, they always asked me afterwards if I felt "cooler." What I noticed, mainly, was that it stung, but I didn't say anything, I didn't want to spoil their enthusiasm. They washed my privates, too, but with plastic gloves, I kid you not, it didn't do anything for me.

Other than that, for two days the weather had been fine, exceptionally hot, a real furnace, even for the season. No thunderstorms, I was sweating like a pig on the plastic undersheet, and I thought about my fields, shit . . . I could have done the hay, normally. I hoped Ramón would begin with the fields on the slope, that's where it always ripens first. But he knew better than me.

I told him not to come and see me, I wanted him to take care of my fields, and I didn't want him to realize that I was sicker than I was letting on. He knew me inside out, and it was obvious to me that he would have it all figured out. You don't slice a guy in half for pleurisy.

As far as my case was concerned, I didn't understand a thing, even though they explained it all as if I were a half-wit. I had become illiterate. There was nothing to be done, it just would not register, I could not make heads or tails of their medical jargon. It was happening to someone else, I would watch myself eating, pissing, walking down the corridor, and I felt like I was in a movie, observing some other guy who was going through what I was going through: he was good at it, this guy, he was a good actor. He'd get the Oscar for best cancer patient.

I even smiled when I saw myself in the mirror, naked, smeared all over with Betadine, drains hanging here and there, the compression bandage on my torso, it looked like I had amazing pecs. With the scar, I'd be able to tell the girls I'd been a mercenary in Zaire and I'd been wounded with a machete and been knocked out for ages. Thing is, I never spoke to girls.

I left the hospital one morning fifteen days later. That evening, I went to drink an Estrella with Ramón, I almost felt back to normal, physically, just a little slow on the uptake, with a faint, foggy sensation that I chalked up to anesthesia. I was praising modern medicine to the skies and I figured that, really, there's no end to progress. Ramón got plastered, I was tempted to do likewise to forget all that anxiety, but I had to be reasonable, all the same. I just bummed a cigarette off Felipe, and it had the same effect as a joint. Fortunately, Ramón was already drunk, otherwise I suppose he would have lectured me like he'd done that afternoon, when I had bummed a Ducados off him.

I propped him up to take him home to old Edelmira, his landlady, I still had some strength, the old man must have weighed at least a hundred and fifty pounds and he was leaning on me, shamelessly, on the opposite side from where they'd operated. I was just careful he didn't get near my scar, which still hurt. He was dribbling down my neck, the jerk, and telling me he loved me. But just after that, he murmured, "My filthy little bitch."

When I went back to Don Confreixo's for the medical leave business, some papers to fill out, he didn't say anything, just that he'd received the report on the operation.

He was holding it in his hands, the sheet folded in three, and he was reading.

I waited absently, slightly groggy the way I'd been all week. I was staring at a fly that was running across the pile of files behind him. I don't know why she swallowed the fly. A vague little smile. He was serious, still reading.

My gaze landed on the letter, and upside down I could read the first part, the upper third, down to the fold. It was too far, I could only read what was typed in bold: *Tomás Lopez Gabarre*, and then two lines further: *non-small-cell carcinoma, stage IIB, T2N1M0*. Something like that. But all I remembered was *Tomás* and *carcinoma*.

It was a slap in the face. A nasty punch to knock your head off your shoulders. I was that fly from a few minutes before who'd just been swatted with a great almighty whack, squashed, dead, just my legs still twitching on reflex.

I can't remember what happened at the appointment after that, I just remember leaving his office, and finding myself in the street. A sensation of falling, slow motion. I was terrified, I looked at the passersby, the few cars in the street, the morning bustle. This life that suddenly I no longer belonged to. All those people who didn't know I was going to die, in terrible agony, for sure. I felt like screaming. Cancer, fuck. Cancer. It was as if I'd understood, all of a sudden: the disease was in my head, I'd just had it tattooed on my forehead. I understood that up until now I had totally blocked out the news, that I'd buried it in the depths of my brain without analyzing it, because it was too harsh, too unfair. I'd been stunned, pinned against the wall, I'd cloaked myself in denial to be able to go on standing, not to crumble like a pile of shit, not to roll around on the ground and weep like an old woman. To be able to go on living, as simple as that, and push away death, because it had come to kiss me on the neck and whisper sweet words. Cancer, for real, for me, inside me, playing against me. I finally realized the impact of anxiety, the fear that was pulling my legs out from under me, the anger making my heart beat faster, the sadness bringing tears to my eyes.

I motioned to Ramón, who was waiting for me at the bar with a beer. He came running over. I murmured:

"Take me home, I have to get some rest."

I couldn't go home alone with this thing.

The old man understood, he looked at the toes of his shoes.

"I'll come with you if you don't mind, kid. I have a back-ache just now, I'd like to get some rest myself. Last few days we've been working like Moroccans without papers."

*

The days that followed, I had to go on living in spite of everything, go on sleeping, eating, working. Taking the time to do a thousand and one everyday things. At the supermarket in Lugo when I got to the checkout, I felt like screaming at all these clueless people that I had cancer. Then I tried to work out how many of us in the crowd were sick with it. I'd been told ten percent. I counted ten in the crowd, so there must be one like me. I would surely recognize him. He would look sad, sick, defeated. I murmured, "Where are you, my brother in pain?"

I didn't find him. We didn't have the same tattoo artist.

I had to keep quiet, to avoid people going on and on. I couldn't have stood it if someone started telling me to keep my spirits up, I would've smashed their head in. All the same, I was afraid. This huge fear, the kind that leaves you paralyzed, fossilized, your legs like cotton.

Weird stuff started happening to me once I was living with my cancer buddy: I could not see an old man without feeling a rush of rage. I hated white hair, toothless mouths, bodies twisted with arthritis, because I knew I'd never have them. Those old people were alive, whereas I was going to die, and I was barely forty. The glaring injustice of it. Those old people complaining, on and on. Who knew everything about everything. Who judged you according to when they grew up, or unloaded their pathetic lives and their two-bit experiences on you as if they were laws of nature. I wanted to steal their memories, the time they had remaining. Their retirement, if they were so afraid of losing it.

I was jealous of their old age and it no longer frightened me, I wanted it, I envied it. I wanted gnarly hands and a past, I wanted rheumatism when it's about to rain. I wanted grandchildren to bounce on my lap, and a walker to go buy my bread. I wanted to shit in my diapers, and annoy the caregivers at the retirement home, and play card games and chew on my false teeth. I ardently desired all the pain, the compromises, the petty little joys in reward for a life of labor. I was entitled to them, just like everyone else. More than everyone else, maybe.

Only old Ramón found favor in my eyes. And always because he knew how to keep his mouth shut.

With churches, same thing. I couldn't see one without wanting to set fire to it and throw stones at the stained-glass windows. Over and over I recited the lines of that French poet, whose name I have forgotten: *And at night we hurled arrows at the stars [. . .] On the door we carved: God, keep out.*

God? He'd forgotten all about me, the bastard.

Bullshit.

And yet it was on a day like any other that I saw her for the first time. I turned my head toward the bar and saw this woman.

The seconds tolled in my head, one by one, with the intensity of a bell. Desire welled up in me, like a raging wind announcing hail. My heart was swelling, unrelenting, all alone and stifling in my chest that was suddenly too small. What I had left in the way of lungs had vanished, collapsed somewhere, since I couldn't breathe.

I closed my eyes, felt like I was about to pass out, desperate for air.

"Hey! Kid? You all right? Tomás?"

The old man's voice calmed me down a little. I took a huge draw on my cigarette, to see if I could still breathe, to check whether I was still alive.

"Yeah, yeah. Don't worry. It's almost too cold in here, compared with the sun outside. I don't feel too good. Must be the antibiotics making me feel tired. Don't worry about me. Don't worry, I'll be fine."

I said it again, as if to convince myself.

"You gave me a fright, kiddo! Even under your dark skin, you're as green as an almond. And fuck it, can't you stop smoking?"

"I told you, it's the fatigue. I'll take a nap. Too late to stop smoking."

"Yeah, you're right, go on ruining your health, kid, never mind what I say . . . "

I smiled like a half-wit, a broad grin. I knew it wouldn't take much effort to get the old man to leave me alone. The only thing he cared about here was the television. Once my smile had reassured him he went back to watching the news. The old man worshiped the huge flat screen, the only luxury in the bar with its smoky walls. It was his drug, his coke, he snorted it every day at noon, injected his pupils with the anchorwoman and her blood red painted lips and her impeccably round breasts in her tight-fitting designer blouse. The news, as usual, churned out its daily load of misery, fear, and injustice, but the old man didn't give a fuck because it was all in high definition color.

So I was able to inspect the woman again, a few yards away from me. I was almost afraid to look at her. I let my gaze slip slowly to the left, afraid she might have disappeared, or would appear completely different, something like that. She wasn't aware that I was looking at her, with a damp cloth she was slowly wiping the long coppery surface of the bar on the customers' side: I could see all of her.

She was leaning slightly forward, I could just make out the top of her white, rather heavy breasts, her delicate milky skin hidden beneath the light cloth of her dress. Her hair, strawberry blond, fell in loose curls around her face.

She had the big empty eyes of a slightly stupid dog, but

what saved them was that they were the bright blue of a summer day. Lips parted slightly with effort, moist, a delicate, pearly pink. Either because of her small size or extreme pallor she seemed fragile. There was something exaggeratedly feminine about her, too sweet, too pale, which filled me with a furious desire to grab hold of her, shake her, slap her, and, in the end, possess her. Possess her. Fuck her, in other words. But hit her, first.

I got a painful hard-on, stuck in my trousers. I wanted to moan. I was trying to contain myself, I raised my eyes to the ceiling and tried to breathe more deeply without attracting Ramón's attention. I stretched out my legs to relieve the tension in my cock, I crossed my arms, took a sip of beer, bent my legs nervously, and started the whole process over again. I was sweating like a pig, I could feel the sweat trickling down my back and inside my thighs. I wished I could have bellowed. I took it out on my cigarette, crushing it hard in the ashtray. For a few seconds, I toyed with the idea of putting it out on my hand so the pain would take my mind elsewhere.

"What is wrong with you? Would you stop fidgeting? You're like a kid who's got worms," said Ramón, worried all of a sudden.

"Fuck off, watch your TV. I've got cramps in my legs."

I could not take my eyes off her, and yet I knew I could have sensed her moving around the room without even looking at her, just from the vibration, the air moving, the murmur of her gestures.

Álvaro, the owner, came to my rescue. He emerged from the kitchen with his traditional platter of sandwiches, Serrano ham, and sheep's cheese.

"Well, guys? Now that you've got time, how are things?"

As usual, the old wreck was dressed to the nines. His baby pink shirt, with a white collar and pinstripes, was stretched tight over his imposing paunch. His sleeves, turned up at the wrist, showed off his flashy jewelry. A watch: square face with a wide crocodile wristband, Roman numerals, the day's date and a second hand. A triple chain in solid gold as heavy as handcuffs; a signet ring with his initials devouring an entire phalanx of his left ring finger. On his chest, same story: a huge gold pendant with Christ on the cross swinging from left to right over the curly, still-black hair on his chest. This guy was a walking jeweler's shop, and a commercial for a hairdresser's: his slicked-back white hair cascaded in oily curls to the base of his neck, while his irreproachably thin mustache, embroidered with pointed scissors into a shadow of froth, looked like nothing so much as a discreet line of beer foam. In his wake, he left a heavy scent of cheap aftershave, not unlike high-end air freshener for a toilet.

Álvaro was fond of me, basically. Other than Ramón, whom I always paid for—I was his most loyal customer. We ate there every day at lunch, and sometimes in the evening if we'd worked late. We often stopped by during the day for a drink. I had my own bottle, a good Rioja aged in an oak barrel. He charged way over the actual price for it, but I knew he ordered it for me alone and that no one else had the means to pay for a wine like that. Life was tough in these parts, we were far away from everything, we lived in almost complete autarky. We were used to doing without virtually everything, and to living frugally. The smallest piece of meat, the tiniest octopus were virtually priceless. Generations under the yoke of poverty, and a financial crisis that had broadsided us added another layer of difficulty. The hardship had dug in, we were like stones surprised by a winter frost. The most striking thing was that since we were used to doing without, and couldn't deprive ourselves any more than we already had, we'd become sparing even in our feelings and our relations with others. We didn't say much, just what was essential, indispensable. We kept to a bare minimum.

We didn't know how to deal with gentleness. Our values had not changed—friendship, honor, love, respect—but we only expressed them in deeds, and they too were reduced to an extreme. Words had disappeared. Happiness was fleeting, almost a miracle, and often culinary. A good glass of wine, a good plate of meat, a dark bread that stuck to your guts were more satisfying than any compliment. Poverty hadn't made us mean, but it left us close-fisted when it came to feelings. I should have been more talkative, since I was richer, but alas, I was even more rough around the edges than the others, because I had constructed myself with this lack of love, and no one had been able, or had had the time, to teach me otherwise.

Staring at Álvaro, examining him from every angle, was entertaining, and it was good for me. I could get my attention off that woman.

"Hey, guys? I asked you how you're doing? Would it make your lips fall off to answer sometime, today?"

"We're fine, Álvaro, we're fine, don't get carried away . . . "

Ramón didn't even look away from the television.

"Okay, okay."

I nodded, making a superhuman effort to concentrate.

"Done with haymaking?"

"Are you crazy? We're only halfway done. The tractor's broken down, and I've had pleurisy, so we've fallen way behind."

I didn't feel like talking, in the end. My words came out reluctantly, I just wanted Álvaro to be quiet and move over, he was blocking my view of the woman.

"Sit down, Álvaro. Can I buy you a beer?"

It was the only way to get what I wanted.

He looked at me, astonished. It wasn't really my style, as a rule, to buy people drinks. I had a reputation for being a real miser, and it had stuck with me for years, but you can't be the richest man in the village without making others envious.

He answered, narrowing his eyes, full of suspicion:

"I won't say no. Particularly if it's your treat, we haven't exactly made it a habit. And in this heat, I'm already parched. Future hundred-year-olds like me have to keep hydrated, not a day goes by without them ramming it down our throats on the box."

Ramón was quick as lightning:

"Can you drink beer to get hydrated? Don't forget, we're the same age, you old mummy!"

Álvaro swung around toward the woman and shouted, "Suiza!"

She slowly turned her head to look at him. Her face was expressionless, if she hadn't moved you might have thought she was deaf, dumb, and blind.

"A beer!"

Álvaro was shouting. He articulated every word as if he were spelling them.

"Why are you shouting? Is she deaf?"

He turned back to me.

"No, but . . . She doesn't speak Spanish. She just understands two or three words, like 'hello,' and 'wine,' 'sleep,' and 'eat.' Mind you, that's plenty for a woman, isn't it?"

He laughed very loudly, holding his belly, proud of his joke.

She disappeared into the kitchen. Then I could concentrate on the conversation.

"She's your new waitress?"

"Yeah . . . Well, waitress, I suppose, yeah. She's not too bright, all the same. Paula brought her to me. She found her in her chicken coop. Filthy and starving. Apparently, she'd been sleeping in there for a while."

"Where's she from?"

"Switzerland, apparently. That explains the name. In fact, we don't even know her name. Some Swiss name, probably, something not from around here. But everyone calls her Suiza.

That way, she's a bit more local, you see. Although . . . . With her coloring, even in Galicia, she wouldn't fool you for long."

Álvaro started laughing again, a belly laugh, which distracted Ramón from the television, and he too got interested in the conversation.

"From Switzerland, you said?"

"Yes, my friend, that's globalization for you! Before, it was our people who left so they could feed their families and work like slaves for a miserable salary, but now it's the Swiss who come to Galicia to make their fortune."

"If the Swiss have come to make their fortune with you, Álvaro, they're not nearly there yet!"

Ramón started chuckling, too, like a turkey, slapping his huge strangler's hand on the other man's shoulder. A fine pair of senile old geezers.

The Suiza woman came back to the table with a tray and the beer.

"For just one beer, don't bother with the tray," shouted Álvaro, enunciating carefully.

"Why are you talking to her as if she were retarded?" asked Ramón.

"Hey, old man, you should listen up when I'm talking! She doesn't speak Spanish. You can tell her to her face that she's stupid, she doesn't understand. You can insult her, she doesn't budge. The ideal woman, I tell you."

And indeed, she didn't understand. Besides, she wasn't listening. She wasn't even looking at us, she was absorbed with what she was doing: putting down the beer, the glass, careful not to knock them over. She was nibbling at her lower lip with little white baby's teeth.

I was going crazy, I could feel it. Because of her smell, now, wafting over me. A simple mixture, sensual and odd, of faint sweat and milk. A floury, sugary woman's scent long gone from my memory. Closer up now I could see her blond hair, veering toward a definite red. Not the long black cascading locks of the village girls, which they pinned up in a chignon or in some complicated construction of sturdy curls and stray locks; this woman's hair was absolutely delicate, falling in soft waves all around her face. I could just make out her ears, which were small, too, and the base of her neck, throbbing with a clear blue network of veins.

I was going berserk, once again. A predator. I wanted to bite her where her veins were pulsing, and only let go of her neck once she'd finished struggling. I recalled a scene like that, a fox suffocating a quail, the sparkling chill in its patient, determined eyes.

I stood up, in slow motion, very calmly, to surprise her, grab her as quickly as I could. I was at least three heads taller than her, it would be easy. I stared at her so intensely that she eventually looked up at me, at last, once the beer and the glass had been set down without mishap. She seemed to be instantaneously afraid. I felt that she could sense my desire, my power, and that I frightened her. Her fear made her even more immobile, my gaze nailed her to the spot.

Neither one of us moved an inch, knowing that the first one to make a move would precipitate an attack or an irreversible flight. I was in the starting blocks, ready to spring forward.

"Hey! Beat it!"

Álvaro's shout fell like an ax on the moment that was bringing us together. I realized he had repeated his order for perhaps the third time already. I chickened out. So did she, she suddenly realized, and turned around ridiculously fast, as if the devil were at her heels, and she charged over to the bar, walking like a robot.

"She really is thick," sighed Álvaro. "But hey, she's good at housework. And the rest, too," he added, winking knowingly at Ramón.

"You're fucking her? Fess up, Álvaro, are you fucking her?"

"A little. She doesn't mind."

Bastard. An old guy like him!

Then, looking up at me, "Where are you off to?"

It's true, I was on my feet. I had to get out of there. I couldn't stay, she might come back.

"I have to go. I have things to do. Put it all on my tab, as usual."

"Already? But kid, didn't we just get here? Aren't we eating today?" asked Ramón, anxious.

"I made cod, I'm sure you'll like it."

"I have to go. You can stay, have lunch, and meet me after siesta, when you like. I have an errand to run."

"Ah! Okay. You're the boss, kid, I haven't forgotten, but there's work, then there's the stomach, see. A good worker is a worker with a full stomach."

Then, turning to Álvaro:

"Cod is fine by me. What have you got with it?"

"I've got some little Marta potatoes for you, the ones that grow over by the bridge, nice and tender."

"Perfect! You can go, boss, I'll stay with Álvaro."

No sooner had I turned to go than Ramón started up again:

"Álvaro, you old goat! Tell me, since we have time. And change the channel, so I can see those American clips with tall black guys wearing necklaces and little chicks in hot pants. After that you can call your illiterate waitress for another beer, just for a laugh. And while we're at it, tell her to bring some olives and a few *pinchos*, I'm still waiting for them. Don't they get olives, in Switzerland, along with their beer?"

I could have killed the pair of them, just to let off some steam.

I cleared out of there. I climbed onto my tractor, set off like a shot, and drove home, swaying with the ruts, lulled by the sound of the engine. I was muttering all sorts of disconnected things, leaning forward slightly, hanging onto the steering wheel. I wasn't myself.

It was the dog, barking with joy, which roused me from my internal monologue. I'd already been in the farmyard for a moment, the engine was switched off. I gave him a brief caress, since he was glad to see me back, then without a glance at the rest of the house, four at a time I climbed the stairs—first stone then wood—that led up to the attic. Amid the spiderwebs there was a little window that looked out onto the surrounding countryside. It was my watchtower. Even as a little boy I would hide here when my father had scolded me for some childish prank. I had placed an old stool under the little square of sky and now I sat there smoking, my head in the skylight. From my observatory, the view encompassed my entire Galician countryside. Fields as far as the eye could see, like a soft green ocean swell, like the sea itself, not far from here yet invisible. The eucalyptus trees, blue gums. The tender blue color of the young leaves, the dark green coming later. When the morning wind got up and made the forest sigh, it was as if there were two colors in one. Blue or green. Green or blue. Depending on the strength of the wind, it was always different. If the breeze stirred the leaves just a little, it was like a great school of terrified anchovies, fleeing before the fishermen's nets, when their sparkling bellies would catch a ray of sunshine. If the breeze became wind, then the entire forest would howl, and powerful waves of two colors, full of foam, would roll through the big branches and over the treetops to crash against the sky. I particularly liked the thick leprous eucalyptus bark, peeling off in great perfumed scales to reveal the new skin beneath, fresh and luminous. I knew the sound of the dried leaves beneath my boots and the crackling of the little lanterns the tree's fruit resembled. I told myself I ought to go out there that afternoon, that it would do me good to see my plantations. A few hectares, for wood pulp. It was always wrenching, when it came time to chop down one of those colossal trees, but I cut them anyway, because they were ogres devouring everything in their path—oaks, pines, centuries-old chestnut trees from the original forest.

As a rule, the sight of my countryside filled me with power, a sense of possession, of pride that filled me to the brim. I'd been able to stay at home, I hadn't needed to go to Buenos Aires like my grandfather, father, and uncle—like most of the men in the village, those ancestors who had left me their land and the freedom to choose, the ease they had not known. But that day, there was nothing under the blistering sun, in the surrounding beauty, that could satisfy me. I felt smothered by desire, taut as a drum, uncontrollable. I had never been in such an agitated state.

I hadn't had many women in my life, all things considered. They'd always frightened me. Ever since adolescence I hadn't been able to speak to them. But I didn't speak to anyone, basically, I felt lonely and lost in a world that was too big for me. The others made fun of me all the time, but not within earshot, since I was fortunate enough to be taller and bigger than everyone, already, and I had a reputation for being something of a hothead.

At secondary school, and then during my higher education, my entire social life consisted of talking day and night with my computer, and finding satisfaction in intense sessions of masturbation. The only thing that was transcendent was running. I ran every day for at least two hours. It was magical, I could forget myself. I ran slowly, but steadily, and my power was my endurance. There was, more than anything, that impression of absolute pleasure, after long minutes of effort, when I was able to put my brain on "off."

Back then I had only a few friends, cretins like me, pimply and ill at ease. When we met up, we never had any of those long conversations where you remake the world: it was enough just to drink beer and spend all night in realistic, violent role-playing.

I got into the habit of drowning my solitude and my inability to communicate in fountains of booze. I was drinking a dozen beers a day just to feel more or less normal, and during the numerous student parties, by ten P.M. I was already dead drunk in a gutter, on the verge of an alcohol-induced coma. Even drunk I wasn't funny. Naturally, none of the girls were interested in me, because they took me—rightfully—for a taciturn, unattractive alcoholic with about as much charisma as a slotted spoon and the finesse of a trailer-truck.

Once I'd returned to the village, physical labor and managing the farm cured me somewhat of my addiction. I worked relentlessly, drank less, and life seemed easier. Since I felt better, I suddenly decided I would get married, the way I decided to buy a tractor. Agustina, my nanny, found her for me, fulfilling her role as matchmaker to perfection. After spreading the word among all her old acquaintances that I was in the market, she personally vetted all the candidates and chose Rosetta. The unofficial contract was clear: I had land, livestock, and money; Rosetta was a virgin, orphaned, uneducated, without income; she was thrifty and a good housekeeper. Rare qualities, in Agustina's opinion. I was reassured by the simple fact that the girl was a virgin: this meant that if I was useless, she couldn't compare me with anyone else.

The wedding night was a real fiasco, I was drunk by eleven o'clock—a record for me—and I woke up in my vomit at six in the morning to go milk the cows. I tried to consummate my marriage a little bit later, with the impression I was "getting down to work." Already I had trouble getting hard, and Rosetta's terrified gaze ended up making me lose it altogether.

It took me four or five glasses of wine to get up my courage. I have memories of painful penetration, laborious ejaculation, and fleeting pleasure.

With time and habit our sexual relations improved to a degree, but neither one of us found the bliss or pleasure the books described. Fairly quickly Rosetta indicated her lack of enthusiasm. Since I hadn't been able to give her the child she had been hoping for, and her womb remained hopelessly empty, she lost no time in making the sessions of this unpalatable game less frequent. And since I wasn't getting anything out of it either, I didn't complain. We made do with very little, a few quick mandatory monthly relations during her fertile period, for the sake of hygiene and a potential heir. I'd gone back to my sessions of solitary pleasure, regularly confirming the old adage, if you want something done right, do it yourself.

Rosetta died after five years of marriage from a brain tumor. Cancer, even then. Maybe that was why I was so frightened now. All the more so as my only memories of her, unfortunately, are of her last days—her decline, her suffering. At the beginning of the illness the tumor that was eating her head made her do strange, almost poetic things.

In the village, they thought she was going crazy, like her mother, who had ended up in the psychiatric hospital in Lugo. She would get lost in the warren of little streets, take lettuce leaves from gardens that did not belong to her, wash her entire body, fully clothed, in a drinking trough in the middle of a field while the cows looked placidly on. Sometimes she would insult people for no reason, then walk for hours on end, murmuring to herself, to end up collapsed in a ditch where she slept until morning. I would head off to look for her when I got back from milking, shouting her name half the night in the hills and forests, along the paths. I always found her, exhausted, asleep, wet with rain or the morning dew. I had trouble waking her, she would lash out at me with her fists, blindly, still half asleep, and it took me hours to drag her home. We walked along the paths, I was tired and glum, dripping with rain, tense from the effort; she was half naked in the wet dress clinging to her skinny body, and she tried to fight me off to run away God knows where.

After that, it was the pain that gnawed away at her thoughts, despite the sedatives, the morphine. I wanted her to die. I could not stand seeing her anymore, deformed by suffering. I hated her grimacing face, her protruding eyes, her inaudible murmuring, and above all her tall emaciated body, yellow and fetid. It was repulsive, I could not touch her without gagging. When she began to scream day and night, and there was no more hope, I had her admitted to the hospital in Santiago, praying that she would not come out alive, that the Rosetta they would give back to me would be dead and at peace, neatly put away in her coffin, in a white dress and wearing mortuary makeup, and that she would remind me even a little of the woman I had married. The doctors fulfilled my wishes.

While her death was a relief on a practical level, for a long time I felt immensely guilty for not having loved her better, for not having made her happy, and for a very long time I felt I was to blame for her cancer. I told myself that the sickness had attacked her brain because I had not been capable of occupying the terrain, had not known well enough how to get into her mind and her heart, had not known how to cherish her, make a fuss over her, caress her, and ultimately, love her. That the emotional void I had not filled had left room for that maleficent beast, and that even then, once it had settled in, I hadn't known how to get it out of there. What I should have tried then appeared incredibly simple to me: I should have run my hand over the back of her neck from time to time when I sensed she was sad or worried, should have taken her by the hand when we went into the village. Should have touched her for reasons other than just to penetrate her, should have learned about tenderness and gentleness. Should have looked on her with pride. While I could only partially reproach myself for not having made her a mother, I bore the full responsibility for not having made her a woman.

I had not known how to love her, any better than I could love any of the people around me. I thought it would be easy, however, that our shared life would have made relations easier, that I could have learned as we went along, since I hadn't learned how to love as a child or an adolescent. But I had acted the fool. Since I'd told myself from the start that I was useless, I hadn't wanted to evolve. I was delighted to sit at the back of the class and I waited for time to go by, without making an effort. Now that it was too late, I couldn't find any more excuses. I still tried to convince myself that it wasn't just me and my inability to love, I hid behind a constitutional atavism of the male gender. I told myself that this was how men behaved, and that they only became aware of things once they'd happened: they were only really fathers once the kid was born, and they only suffered from absence and solitude once their wife had left them or died. Even if I admitted that I had never truly loved her, I felt her absence cruelly—I could hear her voice in the night, and in the morning when I opened my eyes, I would reach out and touch her cold empty spot in the bed, sadly. I was sorry I had not tried earlier to seduce her, to grow attached to her. The lack of motherly love, the lack of love, period, had made me cold and hard, but that didn't excuse everything. I made a point of going to her grave in the cemetery, and when I was sure I was alone, I would ask her out loud for forgiveness, I told her I missed her, and I promised that in another life we would have a second chance and I'd make it up to her. I asked her to wait for me, because by the time I joined her in death the years would surely have mellowed my soul and my nature, and I hoped, then, to be able to speak to her of love. I expressed my regret that I had not loved her enough, as I had undertaken to do at the church, before men and before God. Sometimes I would cry into my sleeve.

I was not sure she would forgive me.

After Rosetta's death, I occasionally let Ramón drag me down to Lugo, to visit the whores. He had found me a girl from Córdoba, whose name was Nacera, a thin Andalusian with black hair, tanned, dry skin, and flat little breasts with big nipples, like overcooked fried eggs. A woman from Andalusia, in memory of my maternal grandfather, an alcoholic, womanizing gypsy, whose sole legacy to me, when he died of cirrhosis, was the brown skin of a scrap metal merchant, and a love for the guitar and the spirit of flamenco.

I went back to see Nacera from time to time because I needed to, in order not to die of loneliness. I went for the jasmine perfume she sprayed herself with, and which never completely hid the smell of fried peppers and olive oil that accompanied her wherever she went, depending on where you were standing. In the end, I made a habit of going to her. To keep Ramón happy, too, because he thought he was rescuing me from sadness and boredom by taking me on wild adventures, which in fact were nothing more than a few glasses of red wine, some quick intercourse, and a good dose of melancholy. I could only get it up half the time, and I always needed alcohol to improve my pitiful performance. Nacera had sex to make ends meet, in her tiny apartment; she fucked as if she were clocking in at some factory. She would throw a big lemon-yellow towel with a tiger's head motif onto her bed to keep off the stains, then she undressed very quickly. She didn't really enjoy it either, and didn't know how to hide the fact. Her face was inscrutable, she didn't speak, didn't pretend to sigh. I often thought it felt as if I were screwing a plot of Andalusian earth—dark and arid, burnt by the sun. As if I were plowing in the wrong season, without her wanting me to. She couldn't fight back, she was obliged to yield to the plowshare, but there was no smell, no pleasure, the earth remained dry and wild. She produced nothing, neither wheat nor fruit, just a little rare, sterile grass so that her adversary would still have a faint desire to toil away. I would leave these bouts of lovemaking feeling tired, relieved, and nauseous.

The ride home in the van—a Seat Inca that had seen better days but handled like a Rolls—with a drunken Ramón next to me, fermenting the drool on his lips, only made me feel even more bitter than when we set out.

Most of the time, I preferred jerking off, finding my own relief, watching free porn videos on the Internet, or using a few magazines I picked up at a freeway rest stop, old and dog-eared from too much handling.

I particularly liked this one picture where this girl was posing naked in a perverse little maid's apron that didn't hide a thing, or just what it ought to. To me, she seemed slightly corpulent, even gelatinous, a real pig in the literal sense of the term, particularly because of her big pink nostrils, and her close-set beady little eyes. From behind she was even worse, she had a smooth pink butt, round and shining, and all that was missing was the corkscrew tail. The moments I spent with the girl in the photo also left me feeling more wretched than anything else, but I couldn't totally do without.

I was well aware that what was happening to me now was something completely different. Never before had I felt such a strong desire. I thought of the woman wiping the copper surface of the bar, her breasts, her hair, and instantaneously I got hard, began to sweat, and was overwhelmed with anger. I could not think of her without clenching my teeth.

I picked up my guitar and played a song by Pastora Pavón. An old forgotten flamenco ballad, one I had not sung in ages:

Una farruca en Galicia
Amargamente lloraba
Porque a la farruca
Se le había perdío
Su rebañito de cabras
Arriba el limón
Abajo el olivo
Limonada de mi vida
Limonada de mi amor
Allá arriba, allá arriba
Allá arriba los dos
Después de pasar fatigas . . .

I sang very quietly in the beginning, just to myself. Some more songs followed, and my voice got louder without me noticing, because it was my heart moaning, my loneliness seeping out, my desire languishing. I ended up shouting. I frayed the words, pierced them with exaggerated weeping, and I sobbed, because I was the unhappiest man on earth: hear my pain, see how it is eating me up, devouring me, as if it were annihilating me.

In the sultry noon heat, only the farm could hear, curled up against the forest, troubled, weary, isolated. The lament of the Man. Only the hens hiding under boards to escape the blazing sun of siesta time went on stupidly cackling.

I whined for a good hour in my attic. It did me good, to act the proper gypsy, crushed with pain, innocent, and full of rage.

I went down to the kitchen, I was starving after all. Some chorizo, a piece of white bread, and some Rioja. I drank quickly, a few glasses, to calm down. But I was drinking less those days.

In reality, I wasn't that hungry.

I rolled a cigarette and lit it in the gloom. Through the smoke I had a look at my house, my lair: the dazzling light from outside trying desperately to pierce the darkness of the room, to get in through windowpanes splattered with fly shit.

The table was cluttered with various things—string, tools, forks, oil, and empty cans. Dirty clothes were piled on a sagging armchair, firewood was tumbling from its pile as if to make a staircase. The chairs had broken legs, and the stuffing was coming out. On the dingy shelves, there was a whole display of dying bulls, and an entire garland of peasant souvenirs: old hand-painted plates, the Virgin of Rocío or elsewhere, dusty tapestries, holy images, and twisted bottles. It was filthy. An old bachelor's house. I would end up alone, sick, devoured by my dogs.

Sixteen years since Rosetta died. Sixteen years of solitude. That must be why I was on a short fuse, even with my late-stage cancer. I would turn forty at Christmas, I was still in the prime of life, in spite of my illness. I should have bought myself another wife, another Rosetta . . . Even if old Ramón still called me kid, or son, or boy, time had had its way with me like with everyone. I felt old, worn out, sick, and bitter. And I had been talking to myself for ages.

Go on, time for a nap.

My bed. Get some rest before Ramón comes around and we go back to work until evening. The wine had calmed me down a little, my eyes were stinging, and I felt like I weighed two tons.

My bedroom was just the same. Dirty. The thin white polyester curtains were black with grime, and the bedspread was long gone. There were no more sheets, either, most of the time I rolled up in a blanket and that was enough. The night tables were overflowing with everything I would put in my pockets and then empty in a hurry before collapsing on my bed, drunk with wine or fatigue. I hadn't opened the shutters since Rosetta died, I only came here to sleep.

Outside, silence reigned supreme. Just the rhythmic clucking of the chickens, or dogs barking, disturbed in their sleep. Even the large, sharp leaves of the palm tree in the courtyard were still, waiting for the evening breeze to quiver.

I couldn't get to sleep. Eyes closed, I was mulling over the emptiness of my pathetic life, and my fear that it might end prematurely.

I opened my eyes slightly: my gaze went from one wall to the next, then stopped at the window, where a fly was dying in agony, buzzing in fits and starts on the dirty windowpane. The gray curtains suddenly made me think that Ramón was right, that I ought to find a cleaning woman. I would ask Agustina. The woman at Álvaro's bar burst into my thoughts, her whiteness, her slow gestures. She was the one I wanted, but not to do the cleaning.

I leapt out of bed. Everything came back to her, incessantly. I walked stealthily through my own house, I was going around in circles without knowing what to do, assailed again by my thoughts of her. I went to find a photograph of the naked girl, she looked at me lasciviously with her piggy little eyes. She no longer aroused me, that afternoon she really did resemble a huge sow.

I took a cold shower. I had to get to work, for sure. Work and fatigue would certainly offer better relief than music, where the effect was too fleeting. And in the evening, I would go into the forest.

Go on then, calm down. Take your bromide. Stop talking to yourself, for Christ's sake.

The next day, I had to go back into Lugo for the next stage of the treatment.

I sat in the waiting room of the eminent professor, a renowned oncologist. Don Confreixo had a long arm and I had money, that made it easier to get treatment. My last chance doctor, I figured.

I wondered what could make someone deal exclusively with cancer patients. Maybe he had come last on some list, and only had a limited choice. Proctologist, or cancer specialist . . .

I was a bit tense. This was the day they were going to tell me what fate had in store for me.

I was stifling. There was nothing to read, just magazines as old as the hills, all torn up because everyone had gone off with the articles they liked. It was strange, actually, to think of a woman with cancer, at death's door, pinching the day's recipe, pleased as punch to have found at last the answer to that existential question: what am I going to make for dinner tonight?

Speaking of women with cancer, a fairly nice one came in, with a wide-brimmed hat, and huge colored earrings like little parrots. She had deep black eyes and a gentle smile, *Buenos días, señor, Buenos días, señora*. She sat down and gently placed her hat on the chair next to her, then looked over at me with a certain pride: *she had no hair!*

My smile froze, I must have looked like a scarecrow.

The appointment? A frank explanation about everything that was going to happen to me. I had registration number 2222, they had taken a photo of me with a Polaroid to staple to the file. Maybe after the treatment no one would recognize me? Since the camera was as old as the Spanish Civil War, I was all green in the photo, it was funny. Green and up against the wall, with a faint smile where you could just make out my teeth. Smiling, a mere reflex.

The bigwig explained: chemotherapy, radiotherapy, blah, blah, blah. Between two explanations a pimply intern knocked on the door and apologized. He was there about a hopeless case. He was whispering in the big boss's ear, but I could hear everything. A man who was dying, the tests were appalling, terminal stage, pain and analgesics. I was shaking with a nervous, unstoppable laugh, the bigwig looked at me condescendingly, as if to say, "Go on, don't worry, everything's fine, it's normal."

As soon as the intern went back out, he continued his monologue, tossed out his well-oiled spiel. Hair will fall out, burns with radiotherapy. Yadda yadda.

"I'm frightened, Doctor."

"That is perfectly normal, young man. We have a psychologist at your disposal who specializes in working with cancer patients, she will certainly be able to help you. Do not hesitate to get in touch with her."

And what I heard was: it's normal, asshole, to be frightened when you know you're going to die, but I don't have time for your metaphysical questions, I still have thirty or more patients after you, so if you could shift your little behind off the chair and get out, quick, I still have a ton of work. If you want to let it all out, there's a specialist in cancer patient whining, the psychologist, who will set you straight. *Next?*

I got home early that afternoon, I was able to head straight for the fields without stopping off at Álvaro's, I didn't want to run into Suiza.

But no matter how I tried to focus my mind elsewhere, it kept going back to her. I drove mechanically in the baking mid-afternoon sun. I followed the swath like a zombie, constantly thinking of her, the woman at the bar. Again, I saw the slow movement of her white arms, could smell her perfume. Suddenly I just let it go, I couldn't fight it anymore, I was wearing myself out trying to forget her. I got a slow, mellow hard-on, nothing nervous.

I made my decision, it fell like a blade of clarity. Anyway, I didn't have the sort of time ahead of me for flourishes. In the end, I would go to the bar, that evening, to smell the woman again. The prospect reassured me. I would go that evening. My lips were like a bloodthirsty beast's, curled back from my white teeth into a smile I hoped looked fierce. It wouldn't have taken much for me to crane my neck and scream my lungs out with all my rage and desire.

I decided that I would go to Álvaro's that evening in good conscience. I had a plan worthy of a contract killer, simple and precise, methodical. I would see her, wait for her to go out, corner her, and fuck her.

Maybe even in front of everyone.

I don't know how to tell things, because I've been stupid ever since I was little, everyone says so. I don't know how to talk very well either. I can't count at all, numbers are too hard. Sometimes I can make sentences that are more or less correct, but that's because I remember them, I have a good memory. That's the only thing I'm good at, memory. I remember other people's words, normal people's words. Like for example, my friend Cindy or Madame Laurent, the teacher, or Madame Bobillier, the psychologist. My Papa's sentences. He didn't speak well either and he repeated a lot, so it got in my head and now it won't come out.

The whole thing began, I think, because I wanted to see the sea.

When I decided to leave, my name was still Sylviane. The sea was so as to erase the snow, because I couldn't stand it anymore, especially in the morning. I always woke up too early, the number was 5, five o'clock. When it's by itself, it's easier. It's when there's something afterwards that I don't know anymore.

That's me all over: I begin a story and I end up telling another one, and then I can't remember exactly what it was I wanted to say.

I was saying that when I got up—always too early—when I saw the snowplow go by, and the snow was falling in big cottony flakes and I was drinking my coffee with my forehead against the cold, damp windowpane, I felt sad. I felt so alone, more than anything.

Even if I switched the radio on that wasn't enough. I became convinced that if I could have heard the sea from my bed, with the waves, even at night, it would have spoken to me.

In the home, I was always cold. I had breakfast under my blanket and I looked at my room. It was small but it was clean, I liked doing housework, it calmed me down. I had everything I needed, even two plates and two glasses. Two, so I could have a guest, but no one ever came to eat with me.

I hated the walls, they were sad and dirty, there were thumb-tack holes from the people who were there before, and marks from where furniture had banged them, or fists. Papa also used to bang the walls when he was really annoyed with Maman or me.

I had two pictures, to make it pretty. "St. Peter's Gate in the Snow," and "Fujiyama" a beautiful blue mountain with a white head and in front of it, some pink branches of cherry trees in bloom. At the bottom of the frame it said: "With the Compliments of the Marguet Establishments." "This is a Japanese print," the social worker told me. "Yours is kind of faded, but it's very peaceful all the same."

The hardest thing there was the noise. You knew everything that was going on next door in Laurence's room, or on the other side in Johnny Faivre's, across the way at Mouloude's, and all the others. The noise when they made love or when they fought, or were drinking. No matter what they did, they always ended up shouting. I thought about Papa every time, and it would've been better if I could have managed not to think about him anymore. Madame Bobillier, the psychologist, told me that it was the inti-macy of other people's bodies that shocked me, I didn't really understand what she meant. She advised me to try to think about something else. So, I went to get my music, I put my head in my arms and thought about the sea. For music, I had a CD player, and a gorgeous pair of pink headphones, I didn't pay for them, it was Cindy who stole them for me from the Hyper U, for my birthday. The music that calmed me down was Spanish guitar. My favorite track was called Asturias. I really wanted to thank the gentleman who played: Isaac Albéniz. I thought that was a funny name, Isaac, I didn't know anyone with that name. I just knew one Mouloude, some Kevins, some Jordans, one Johnny, one Teddy. If Cindy were here she'd say, "Hey, don't start listing the entire home, who cares who you know." She was always saying to me, "Sometimes you really get on my nerves when you act stupid, for fuck's sake. Use your head."

I could listen to it all day long, fifty times a day, that music. Well maybe not fifty . . . I don't know exactly how much that is, fifty. I made up a story, to the music, a story that made me dream. I tried to tell it to Cindy but she said, "Fuck, what you been smoking, sweetheart, that music of yours does nothing for me, I'd way rather listen to AC/DC."

I don't know where I was again. Oh, yes. I decided about the sea, just like that, one day when it was snowing nonstop.

I took a shopping bag that said "Hyper U Thanks You," and some clothes, and shampoo, and the CD player, and my music. I didn't have a suitcase, I've never been anywhere, other than the day at the Catholic charity.

I had to leave before daybreak, at the home they for sure wouldn't want me to leave just to go see the sea, when it was already super complicated just to go downtown.

I walked to the roundabout on the way out of town, there was no one. I hitchhiked. I was lucky, the first car picked me up. A woman, who was on her way to work in Besançon. She talked a lot, and told me it wasn't a good idea for a young woman to hitchhike at night, there were perverts everywhere. I wondered what that was exactly, a pervert, it must've been some sort of werewolf because that woman looked like she was really frightened.

I remember that night very well. The woman put the heating

on full blast, the radio on quiet, and through the window I could see the trees with their branches covered in snow and looking like they were about to break: the road was like a white tunnel. I peered into the woods to see if I could see the eyes of the perverts, they must shine in the dark.

The woman had almost stopped talking, she was concentrating on the slippery road. She asked me, "Where exactly are you going?" I said, "I'm going to see the sea." She laughed and she gave me a funny look. She must've thought I was crazy, but it was true, I was going to see the sea. She left me in the center of town, it was starting to get light.

I walked for a long time through the streets, I couldn't find which way it was to go to the sea, no one knew where it was. I asked people and they laughed and said, "Is this some kind of joke?" Or they hurried away and didn't answer. I was cold, I was crying, and I thought: "There goes my trip to the sea."

All I did was think about Papa who always said, "Stop sniveling, stupid, and make an effort, how hard can it be, two plus two. If you don't answer, I'll slap your face, and that will get your brain working, who the hell went and brought such a blockhead into the world? Your mother, I suppose."

I sat down on the bench so that I could cry in peace and take out my music. I couldn't see a thing because of all my tears. When I looked up from my bag, this little girl was staring at me. She asked me why I was crying, I said I was looking for the sea and didn't know which way to go.

The little girl knew. She went there every year, to the sea, in Spain. Spain! Like Asturias, like Isaac. I told myself it was a sign and that everything must be wonderful there.

"And which way is Spain?" The little girl told me I had to go first to Lyon, since her daddy always said they could stop and go pee after Lyon. She gave me loads of advice, "If I were you I would go pee before leaving, because in the bathrooms on the freeway you can't sit on the toilet seat, it's too dirty, my mommy *won't let me. But there's free perfume to put on your hands, and it smells good, like vacation. Mommy doesn't want us to put perfume on our face. After that, we stop in Mornas. There's a beautiful castle like in the Middle Ages and they sell nougat with almonds in the store. We don't buy any because Mommy says it's too expensive and that Daddy is already fat enough."*

Her mother shouted, "Hélène!" and the little girl flew away like a bird, chirping, "Have a nice vacation!"

I hitchhiked and I took the first truck that went by. He was going to Lyon, further down even. The driver said he would find another truck for me to go the rest of the way, not to worry, after Lyon it was all Spanish trucks. I was happy, the truck was blue, with a big smiling yellow sun. The man was Croatish, something like that. His name was Andreas. He wanted to talk because he was always alone in his truck, and he missed his wife and his three kids. I wasn't really listening to him, I was looking outside at the fruit trees in bloom, they were pink all over, and behind them were blue mountains with snowy heads. I said, "I know this place: it's Fujiyama, for real, and brand-new, not like in my room." "What are you going on about, you're a funny sort of girl, I've never picked up a hitchhiker like you. That's not Fujiyama, it's the Rhône Valley, and the mountains of the Ardèche, it says so on all the signs."

I fell asleep in the back, he had a real bed in the truck. I woke up because he was stroking my privates, he wanted to make love. He was trying very gently to see if I would cry out or say nothing. It was normal for the trip, so I let him do it. He didn't smell bad, just a little bit of mild tobacco. He hardly stayed any longer than two minutes, I shouldn't have stroked his butt. I was glad he got it over with quickly, though, I was tired.

After, he just asked me if I wanted a Coca-Cola, or if I was hungry. Oh yes, I was hungry. I ate this sandwich, he wasn't looking at me anymore, he wasn't talking anymore either, he drove, that was all. I slept for a long time, he didn't wake me up,

Spain was a long way, it was nighttime and I couldn't see anything.

He woke me up in the parking lot to pass me on to another truck. "He's a nice guy, you'll see," said Andreas, "he's going to Spain." To some big city, I didn't understand the name, it sounded like Pampers. The second guy was from Holland, he made love too, and bought me a coffee and a croissant. He left me with my bag in the Pampers city, I didn't know which way was the sea, but I was still going in the right direction because I was in Spain. I hitchhiked some more, I saw mountains and big flat fields. I couldn't speak anymore, I didn't understand anything in their language. Papa always said, "And anyway you don't understand a thing, am I speaking French or Chinese?"

I didn't know where I was going, I kept thinking I was about to see the sea on the horizon. I rode for days and days, the men would pick me up, sometimes they made love, and they left me by the side of the road. And then no one took me anymore, I smelled too bad. I was hungry all the time, I would pick vegetables in the fields, eat them raw, I had spent all my guardianship money on bread and ham. I saw people looking at me in a mean way.

There was a big city that was called Léon like Monsieur Girardet. I slept outside or in churches that stayed open all the time. I had to watch out for the police, the "guardia civil," it was written in big letters on their cars, the ones that go fast, with sirens. I hid and waited. I was afraid they would ask me what I was doing there, I couldn't have explained about the sea, I was sure they would send me back to the home. I stopped hitchhiking, I walked very early in the morning, when there was no one around. I found fruit, and things in garbage cans in gardens. I hid, day and night.

I must have been making some progress all the same, the landscape changed all of a sudden. But it still wasn't the sea, it was more like the mountains, damp gentle mountains with green *everywhere. I felt better, it was prettier, it was a bit more like where I was from, and I could hide more easily.*

The last day, I slept in a little garden hut because it was raining. I had a cold and some fever, I didn't see it get light and I overslept. It was the woman who was looking at me who woke me up. She gave me some bread so I ate it quickly without thinking. She said "café" and I understood, so I thought she was speaking French. She took me into her house and gave me some coffee and some big madeleines. Some more bread with ham. I ate everything quickly and she laughed. She said, "Tranquilla, tranquilla." She showed me the bathroom, and the shower, and she gave me a dress for later.

That's how I was first called Suiza.

The old man was waving his arms in front of the tractor, I couldn't hear what he was saying. I opened the window and leaned out.

"What? What's the matter?"

"For fuck's sake, what are you up to? Are you drunk or what? Can't you see where you're going? You already came this way!"

I looked behind me. I was going the wrong direction, lost in my dreams of soft white skin and sex.

"Okay, okay! I'll go back. Sorry."

Ramón went on fussing, but with the noise from the machine I couldn't hear him. I made an effort with the following row before glancing quickly at my watch. Eight P.M. The sun was beginning to set behind the woods.

I was fed up and had other things on my mind.

"Ramón! That's it for today!"

"Now? But there are only three rows left at the bottom!"

"I don't care! I've had enough. And besides, we have to unload, we'll finish tomorrow. I'm tired."

"It's supposed to rain tomorrow."

"I don't care, do you hear me? Let's wrap it up, I've had enough."

Ramón looked at me worriedly.

"What did he tell you this morning, that big specialist? You've been acting weird ever since you got back."

"Don't start, all right? I'm tired, is all."

"Okay, all right, we can stop, hey, you're the boss. For all I have to say . . . "

While I was driving the tractor on the way home, I could feel Ramón's suspicious gaze on my neck and shoulders. He still didn't know about the cancer. I'd pleaded the case for pleurisy like a pro, giving him all the details of my hospitalization, and that's as far as it had gone. I talked about a long, difficult treatment that would oblige me to go to Lugo more often, or even Santiago. I could tell he was wary, I was making too much of it to get him off the track of the diagnosis. I was ordinarily closemouthed about things. Now, because I was bringing out the big guns one by one, he didn't stop looking at me from under his eyebrows. And it was hardly like me to stop work before it was done, there in the middle of the field, when you know that in Galicia, two days without rain are two golden days.

"See you tomorrow!"

I put on a falsely relaxed air, once the last cart was unloaded. I wanted to get rid of him so I could do as I pleased.

"You're not coming for a drink?"

Ramón's surprise caught in his throat, a falsetto squeak, his eyes open wide, lips pursed. I closed the door to the barn as if I hadn't heard him. I was going to have trouble pulling a fast one.

"I get it! Your kids are waiting for you!" grumbled the old man.

I spun around, and suddenly exploded with anger in the face of his insistence:

"You are really determined to piss me off today, aren't you! You want my fist in your face? I'll come if I feel like it, when I decide to. I'm still master in my own house, aren't I?"

The best defense is attack. I marched into the courtyard, hollering, and I yanked the kitchen door open; it was all I could do not to kick it open. I turned around to the old man.

"Stop looking at me as if you've never seen me, get the fuck out of here, and come back tomorrow morning."

"Call Don Confreixo, my friend, you worry me."

He was muttering, looking at me like I was a dog about to bite.

I slammed the door in his face. The bastard could read me better than a book, he could tell I wasn't feeling right. How could I not give myself away to this old idiot who knew me like his own son? And why had I told him no about the bar, since that was precisely where I wanted to go?

I rushed to the door again and yanked it open.

"Ramón! Wait! I'm coming . . . "

The old man was already twenty yards away. He turned around and walked back toward me with the smile of an aficionado going to his first bullfight.

"Ah! That's more like it. I was on my way to get the priest."

It had only just gotten dark; the days were getting longer. The sun set the sky ablaze, like in the days when we'd had the fires. We walked side-by-side to the village and I was thinking that, if the path had led through grass, we would surely have left our trace over the seasons and the years, the way herds do in the hills. We took that path at least twice a day, crossing the clear river and the old Roman bridge, to reach the first houses, which gave us the soothing sensation we were returning to civilization: it was impossible to get as far as the main square without shaking someone's hand or greeting a woman. It was a typical Galician village with a harmonious offering of white houses with little windows and colored lintels that brightened the austerity of the dark stone. Hydrangea bushes, yellow daturas, autumn asters, and giant rosebushes added a final touch to the gray walls, an infinite variety of colors that changed according to the season. The center of the village consisted of a fairly empty square, where the three shrines of our rural life were concentrated: Álvaro's bar, Luis's grocery shop, and God's church. The rest of the village rose in winding little streets toward the hills, and the climbing dwellings seemed to have been brought to an abrupt halt by the eucalyptus forest, which was enormous, superhuman, an insurmountable rampart beyond which another world stretched into the distance.

We were far away from everything, even the national highway passed us by, you had to drive several miles to reach it, and only on days when there were strong winds from the east could we hear its murmur. Trucks, and strangers, only found their way here by mistake. Our distance from everything ensured slowness and tranquility, and sentenced us to a life of seclusion, forgotten by the world.

The village became animated during what we referred to among ourselves as "the women's hour." Twice a day. In the morning, when they came out their doors to wash the stoops with multiple buckets of soapy water and gorse brooms. And at twilight, when the sun had not yet completely disappeared behind the forest, out they came again to water their flowers, nip a failed bud or withered blossom with a sharp fingernail, then finally they would simply sit on a wicker chair to enjoy the last sweet moments of evening. Then the village rustled with conversation, people greeted one another, called from one house to the next to talk about a coming birth, or a recent death, or to peddle a few rumors.

As Ramón and I walked along we overheard a few snatches of conversation, but we didn't stop, we were proud and tall: the men met up in the bar.

When we got there, the room was packed.

Suiza was there.

I could sense her presence. I moved slowly, my head between my shoulders, I wasn't in too much of a hurry to see her, I wanted to smell her first.

"Tomás! Are you in?"

Normally, I love playing cards with Felipe and the others.

"No, I don't have time. I'll have a drink with the old man and then I'm off to bed. It's haymaking, you understand."

My voice surprised me, strong and sure. To let her know.

But she already knew I was there.

She was just in front of me, behind the bar. She was looking at me with her big blue eyes, too dull, her mouth half open.

"Rioja as usual?" asked Álvaro, setting a plate of olives and peanuts on the table.

"No, I'll have . . . Orujo."

"But kid, we haven't eaten."

"I'm not hungry. Have your red and eat if you want. I need something stronger."

"Fuck, Álvaro, our young friend is worrying me. He's not behaving normally. First, he left the fields high and dry, now he's skipping meals, doesn't drink his wine anymore . . . "

I remained stony-faced, unmoving, impervious to the noise and conversation, tense and attentive to the woman's slightest movement. Suiza in my sights, again I took in her pallor, her parted lips, the fine beads of sweat on her upper lip. Her quivering nostrils, her short white neck, veins throbbing. Her light dress, the fabric trapping her breasts, her thin waist. I could not see further down, the bar was in the way, but I dreamt of her sex frothing with ginger like her hair, and her soft thighs.

"Maybe he's in love?"

Álvaro, with a knowing wink, indicated my stare to Ramón.

"Maybe that's it, yeah."

The old man narrowed his eyes, he had just caught on, in a flash of clarity. He detected my restlessness, sensed the tension that had me in its grip. Álvaro's incipient anger, my unpredictability and menace. He could tell that murder was a possible option.

"Maybe you should take the kid to Lugo," spat Álvaro

suddenly, full of hatred. "He's got a screw loose now. Solitude and sickness, makes you lose your head and set your sights on other men's women."

"She's not your woman," I said, through my clenched teeth, not taking my eyes off this Suiza.

Álvaro, at a loss, turned to her. Her blatant passivity, which he took for implicit acceptance, her blue gaze lost in mine, eventually made him lose his temper. Raising his arm, he shouted:

"And you, move your ass, stupid bitch! Back to the kitchen! I'll call you when we need you."

Suiza recoiled, registering his anger, but not his words, nor what she was supposed to do, and she stood there frozen with surprise.

I had understood. In a sort of flash, I stopped the movement of Álvaro's arm, caught it and lowered it violently, and kept it flat on the bar. I could have broken it with the strength of just two fingers. Then I would have smashed his skull against the edge of the bar.

"Leave her alone, you understand?"

I wasn't talking anymore, I was hissing. Silence all through the bar. Conversations stopped, cards were left mid-play, only the dull drone of the television went a little way toward defusing the heavy atmosphere.

"Okay, son, it's okay . . . Come on . . . Let him go."

Ramón gently ran his hand over my forearm, he could feel the tension in my muscles. He was stroking me the way you stroke a restive animal to calm it down. His hand went up to my neck and he patted it gently.

"Come on, boy . . . Let's go sit for a drink over there, where it's quiet. Come on, kid, come on. Bring the olives, Álvaro, and stop getting worked up like that, it's not good for your heart. Come on, guys, everything's okay. Let's go."

After a few endless seconds that felt like minutes, I took my hand off Álvaro's arm, in slow motion, ready to grab him again. While waiting, I stayed static, massive, dangerous. It was my jaw that gave me away, it was twitching at regular intervals, and I couldn't control it.

Time was suspended. My heart was pounding in my head, I didn't really know where I was anymore, or what I had to do.

I couldn't just leave it there. I couldn't think.

Quickly, without warning, like a cat springing, I walked around the bar, grabbed Suiza by the wrist, and led her with me to the door.

No one moved. Men know how to recognize madness, they walk right next to it every day.

The door slammed, we fell into the night. I figured that there would be a few moments of stupor, but then conversations and games would start up again as if nothing had happened. The girl was not from around here, and a man's desire is too essential and eminently dangerous a thing for anyone to dare get in the way.

We walked briskly, with me in the lead, crushing her wrist. I was so much taller than her, she had to take two strides for my every one. She was hesitant, because she couldn't really see where she was putting her feet, and because she had awful shoes, misshapen flip-flops. She was trotting along as best she could behind me, making ridiculous little hops that rang out when her shoe struck her heel. I could just sense a different tension depending on whether she moved forward willingly or held back.

The night entered me like a sharp blade. I was trying to calm the palpitations of my soul, I didn't know why I was holding her so tightly, or what I wanted to do with her, or where I was going. I couldn't read any of the external signs that usually make up my alphabet. Neither the strong smell of the eucalyptus, relieved at last of the day's stifling heat, nor the sibylline sounds of the stream, nor the sound of the bell tolling midnight. I was making my way without landmarks, concentrated solely on my heart, which was beating like a solemn bell, and on the woman I was pulling behind me like war booty.

Suddenly I remembered what I took her for. I wanted to fuck her. I stopped short and turned around to look at her.

In the summer night, she was so light she radiated, phosphorescent like a Holy Virgin. Next to the road there was a field, a huge field of fragrant grasses, I dragged her there and our passage left a furrow through the tall grasses. Then I brought our shadows to a sudden halt, in the middle of the bed of fescue. The moonlight made our hair shine white.

I pulled her down and laid her firmly on the ground. I imagined that it was my gaze that was pinning her to the warm grass, I forgot that the darkness made her blind. I was still holding her wrist, and now I moved it above her head. With my left hand, I tried to undo the little buttons on her dress. Her lips were parted, as always, because I could see her white teeth. With a sort of rage, I put my mouth on hers as if to silence her, but above all to kill her too-powerful femininity, it was exciting me, devouring me. Her little mouth was sweet and soft, I imagined its pinkness inside, my tongue savoring it, it took up all the room, I stopped her from speaking or moaning. My cock hurt, I hated my belt and the buttons on my trousers, all those obstacles I would have to overcome to set it free. I eventually tore open the front of her dress, releasing her breasts, which were even whiter than her neck. They were two melons of moon, but I could not touch them because I would have hurt them. I would have had to take the time, to stroke them gently, kiss them tenderly, and I did not have that freedom. Before all else, she had to be mine. I wanted to penetrate her, subject her, reduce her to nothing. She had too much power over me. I wanted to rape that woman, like a barbarian, to steal her body, before the simple fact of looking at her breasts had time to make me come. I wanted to take her flesh and leave my sperm on it, my trace, perhaps my life. I wanted her never to forget. Fuck, more than anything I wanted her to be mine, in the end. I was nothing but that word, want, want, want again and again, I want you, for God's sake, I want you all to myself.

I removed all the obstacles to my desire, only just lowering my trousers enough to let my painful cock out. I lifted one of her legs, and her soft white thigh filled my hand, warm milk on my dry palm.

She did not struggle, did not try to fight me off. I didn't have time to try to wonder why, and with a sharp thrust I penetrated her at last. It was almost painful, not what I wanted, my orgasm exploded in my brain like the discharge of a rifle. I let out an animal cry, a madman's scream. I came, in a great sob of surprise, I didn't want to, not right away. Not now. *Not now!*

I withdrew quickly, and all at once I heard the night and the blood pounding in my temples. I stood up, closed my fly and said:

"Come with me."

I wanted more.

She didn't understand. She was waiting, patiently, for me to go. She did not try to run away.

Then I was overcome with shame. I realized I had not raped her, she had simply let me. Anyone could have their way with her, she never said anything. Me, or Álvaro, it was all the same to her.

I had been thinking only about myself, my own desire. I had imagined abducting her without ever, even for a fraction of a second, entertaining the simple hypothesis that she might actually want to go with me.

I did up the buttons of her dress as best I could and tried to fix what I had torn, so that she'd look more or less dressed. I wiped her thighs, gleaming from me, with my sleeve, and I pulled down her dress to stifle somewhat the shame still buzzing in my ears. I was beginning to feel some remorse, all the same.

Standing, I repeated:

"You're coming with me," and I fastened my belt buckle, never taking my eyes off her: I was afraid she'd run away after all.

I took her wrist again, pulled her brusquely to her feet and dragged her with me. I held her tightly, like before. I moved slowly, soundlessly, she followed, stumbling on pebbles.

I laughed silently to myself, grinning in the dark. I felt strong, I had won, I didn't care what she was, I was no better. I had taken myself for Carlos Soria, but now I remembered I was just a pathetic yokel.

I knew the way by heart. But I despised the forest that was calling to me, the mist still being born in diaphanous layers, the cross at the junction yellow with lichen and shining in the moonlight. I did not see the fox hiding in the ditch as it crouched down on our approach, sensing that Man might only be passing by, that it was not time for death.

It was a long way, she was stumbling more and more. So, I carried her. It was easy, for me. I was taking a woman home, *my* woman. A Sabine, and in the end, it mattered little what she was.

I left her on the steps, just to open the door that was never locked. I pushed her gently into the room.

The bare bulb on the ceiling was dazzling in its faintness. There reigned an indescribable chaos of shadows, and I didn't leave her the time to study it. I led her into the bedroom, tossed the blanket onto the bed, and sat her on the edge. I slipped down on my knees so I would be level with her. But even like that I was still too tall. The little bedside lamp gave off the dying light of an eclipse. All you could see were the essential things—the bed, the night tables, faces, bodies. I wanted to see her breasts and touch them at last.

Gently, this time, I pushed back her hand, which was holding her torn dress closed. There they were, drooping slightly, with pale pink, almost invisible nipples. Dazzlingly white. I closed my eyes and they were still there on my retina. I placed my lips between them, on the path that separated them, to lose myself. I recalled an image of the child I had been, I remembered honey and milk, and maternal softness. I felt like crying. Sobs were gathering in my throat, like kindling about to crackle in the fire. She ran her hands through my long hair, she understood everything, she knew my great sadness of a man who is going to die. She pulled my lips toward her neck, she spoke to my skin, so long neglected, she sang to me of life going by and time leaving its mark. She instilled me with her softness, her youth, she brought me back to reality, to the man I was now, still capable of drinking, eating, and getting hard. I no longer wanted to destroy her.

I lifted her legs and entered her easily. She was smooth, moist, and warm. Her eyes were wide open, those big, rather dull eyes, so blue and touching. With every thrust I gave her, imperceptibly she lowered her eyelids and her gaze clouded, as if someone had thrown a pebble in a lake. She produced a music that reminded me of my flamenco, all sighing and lamenting, growling and weeping. I closed my eyes, came upon long-forgotten sensations, I could sense burning sand beneath my feet, the sun on my skin, the wind ruffling my hair and stirring up the dust, I was dreaming the long unceasing walk of my maternal ancestors. I listened to the voice of her white body melting into mine, which was so dark. She sang like la Niña de los Peines. I wanted to play her like an instrument until morning but already, as in the grasses, I felt I was about to yield, above all because of her lips, which made me think that she liked this, that she wanted more.

I swore like the damned, tried to forget the purity of her skin, and ejaculated in a long sob of rage and pleasure.

I would have liked for it to last forever.

Daylight appeared behind the shutters, and the roosters had been crowing for a while. Ramón would be here soon. I had a quick shower, she waited in the kitchen. She was patient, saying nothing, her hands behind her back. I showed her the coffee, the water, the coffeepot. She nodded. She seemed quite serene, she looked me straight in the eyes when I spoke to her, she was calm. I was the one who felt crappy. Every time I said something, it was in Spanish, mainly because I didn't know what else to say, I felt awkward, and speaking filled the heavy silence. Over time she was bound to retain a word or two.

I had given her one of Rosetta's dresses, a blue shirtdress with little flowers, because her dress was in shreds. The dress was too big, it sagged under the arms and hung down to the middle of her calves. It was ugly, it made her look like a slut. Later I came up with the idea of tying a piece of twine around her waist for a belt, to adjust the size and raise the hem above her knee. Then it looked better, she looked like a woman. I couldn't let her walk around naked.

Ramón came that morning as usual, because it was a fine morning and he knew like I did that it would only start raining in the evening. He gave a stiff smile when he saw the woman.

"Hello, one and all!"

"Hey, Ramón. Coffee?"

"I won't say no, I need one. I didn't get much sleep last night, you see . . ."

I avoided the subject.

"We have to finish the San Martiño fields today, and everything we mowed yesterday before it rains."

He stood in the doorway waiting for me, his smile hanging in the middle of his face, and his cigarette like a cannon belching smoke. That was all he said, but I knew he was relieved that the coffee, the work, and the morning ritual had not changed, despite her presence, sitting there with her cup.

The two of us went off to work, not looking back. I didn't say goodbye: oddly, I didn't even know whether I ought to kiss her or shake her hand, but I was no longer afraid that she might leave.

They left. I stayed by myself in the middle of the kitchen. I wanted to lie down again, but the bed was really too dirty. I felt like opening the shutters, but I didn't know if I was allowed to. I hesitated and then I thought, never mind, I'll try. Oh! It was so beautiful! Green fields, tall trees, and the edge of the forest was tidy and neatly cut like in those picture books I liked so much as a child. There must have been loads of forest gnomes in there. I know about gnomes because of the neighbor, Madame Turbin. She let me read The Big Book of Gnomes. They're little dwarves, who are kind and have a "penetrating" gaze. They cast spells, spells that do good, because they're good gnomes, they protect you. Sometimes they do stupid things, but they're never mean, it's just because they're mis-chie-vous. I don't know exactly what that means, mis-chie-vous. I'd like to buy a gnome so that he would protect me all the time, I saw some at the grocery store, Luis's place, across from Álvaro's. The one I like best is the little fat one with a pipe and a hat that's all twisted. But I don't have any money and I don't know how I would ask for one. There in that forest so near, I was sure there were gnomes hidden behind leaves and that they were watching me with their "penetrating" gaze as I opened the shutters.

The light came in, it was happy, it hadn't been in here in a long time, I think. There were old abandoned birds' nests hanging from the shutters, it must've been that long since they'd been opened. I pushed the nests very gently, just in case there were *still creatures inside, but no, it was all dead in there. I began by cleaning the windowsill.*

There was this beautiful blue-grey stone beneath the dust and filth.

"Young ladies, I will make you into perfect housekeepers, that is the purpose of your studies," said Madame Laurent. In high school, in the special needs section, for four years. Classes in cooking, sewing, everything to make you into perfect house-wives. Cleanliness in the home begins with the cleanliness of the mistress of the house. Wash at least once a day, "the hot bits": armpits, privates, feet. Pluck any coarse hairs and remove hair under the armpits, up to the knee, tweeze eyebrows, look after your secret garden, be fresh and available when your husband comes home from work.

The window was clean, no creatures and no dust. I dragged the mattress to the windowsill to air it out, but in the sun, it looked even dirtier. The other side was better, you could sleep on it. Sleep or make love. Oh, yes! With him I really wanted to. Maybe he'd like to keep me? I would have to make an effort, not say too many stupid things. But anyway, there wasn't much risk of that, I couldn't speak their language here.

In the wardrobe in the bedroom I found an under-sheet, and some sheets that had been ironed and folded a long time ago, and a big pink blanket, it was so loud, with tassels on the sides and little knots in each corner. It was so ugly that it was funny, I wondered who came up with the idea of making a blanket that color, with all those tassels.

I made a nice clean bed.

The man came home. I couldn't tell on his face whether he'd noticed the blanket, whether he was happy about the clean bed. He was tired, and he fell asleep right away.

I slept for a long time too, and when I woke up, the sun was already low in the sky, and the man had been gone for a while, his place was all cold. I did some thinking. I thought: I'm happy. I closed my eyes and I was still happy. I told myself I had to get up, I had to do some housekeeping so he'd want to keep me with him. But there was a little voice inside that said: don't get up, you never know, when you get up you might be unhappy. I fell asleep again right away.

He was there next to me, I didn't hear him come in. I wanted to find out his name, but I didn't know what to do. I didn't know how to ask in Spanish, "What's your name?" I was a savage here, like ... like Pocahontas! She helped me. I remembered, and I did just like in the cartoon: I put my hand on my chest and said, "Suiza." And then I did the opposite, I put my hand on his chest and looked at him with Pocahontas eyes that said, "What's your name?"

"Tomás."

It worked! I thought about Cindy, she would've been proud of me, she said that sometimes I was not as dumb as I looked. Now I knew the man's name. Tomasse. In France, we would for sure have said Thomas, not pronouncing the "s," like Jennifer's Thomas, the one who used his raspberry toothpaste to shave. Mine, he said "Tomasse," as if he were hissing at the end, it was better, it didn't sound like "tomato," like in French. That was exactly what I liked about it here, just little, simple things seemed kind of extraordinary and complicated. Tomasse, I liked that. I wanted him to keep me. Keep me, please, I'll do the housework, I'll do everything you want, keep me some more. I looked at him and concentrated very hard, and I hoped he could hear Pocahontas again.

The next day when he left I thought, down to work now, I

have to stop sleeping all the time. I started with the window-panes and washed them with a sponge. I started at the top, opening the window wide onto the countryside. Outside it was green everywhere, a green that shines really bright with the dew and makes you close your eyes slightly otherwise you can't see anything anymore, it's as if your eyes were burned. The light splattered the path, the fields, the sky with big moist rays. The mist was having trouble leaving, it wanted to stay a little bit longer, it liked it there in the valley. The hens came to see me, they all gathered outside the farm, and made noise as if they were having a conversation. They were surprised to see me moving, scrubbing, they didn't know me. I was washing, brushing, wiping. Hey, hens, how are you? Not too bad, they said. The windows were all happy to be able to see the sun again pouring so easily into the house.

There were dishes that had been lying around for months, at least. They smelled bad, they were all sticky. I soaked them, washed them, gave them a good wipe, otherwise it leaves streaks. Then I put them away in the buffet, there was plenty of room once it was organized. Beforehand, I'd given the buffet a good wash to get rid of the sticky grease and dust. Madame Laurent would have been proud of me. I put the plates with the plates, the knives with knives, the forks with the forks, the big spoons with the big spoons, and the little spoons on their own, there was no more room. But I didn't like it that way, so in the end I changed it, I put the little spoons with the big ones, otherwise they would've been afraid, and I put the knives on their own. That way it was much better, knives are never afraid, they're knives.

I did the shelves, and the knickknacks that were all greasy and sticky. For the Saints and the Holy Virgins, I gave them a bath in Tomasse's shampoo, I was afraid the dishwashing liquid would be too strong. I didn't let them soak too long because I mixed up the men and the women, and that's not good for saints, *they never make love, they don't like that, it's sinful, said Granny Yvette. As for the bull, after the bath, he was bleeding again, all red and fresh, as if he had his period in his neck.*

Speaking of periods, there must have been a woman here a long time ago, I found an old opened package of sanitary pads, super plus flow, with three drops. I also found some neatly fold-ed dishrags, and brooms, everything you need to clean the house, things men don't buy.

I could go on about it for hours, all the cleaning I did, I worked all day long. I was proud of myself and of the house. Especially the floor: before, it was a potato field. Once I'd washed everything, the little polished tiles sparkled like Christmas, they looked brand-new. I changed the water in the bucket ten times at least. The mop was a ball with long hair, like at Álvaro's, that's all they have in Spain. It's practical, you don't break your back squeezing it out, but it's not as efficient as a Swiss mop. I mean a French mop, what am I saying. "You always say stupid things, my poor girl," said Papa. Stop it now, stop, you know he can't talk to you anymore, that those are just memories.
In the bathroom, I cleaned the tiles one by one with a little sponge and some white vinegar mixed with soap. You could have eaten off those tiles, it was so clean. A toothbrush and a glass for Tomasse, and a glass for me, even if I didn't have a toothbrush. I used Tomasse's. A big glass and a big towel for him, a little glass and a little towel for me. Maman, it was like in Goldilocks and the Three Bears.

After that, I sat down and waited for him to come home.

They implanted the port without general anesthesia, to save on the anesthesiologist, I suppose. I already had a surgeon who'd operated on me there for a benign breast tumor, a few years ago, after my military service. Another top specialist. But he didn't do ports. Dirty work, in other words.

So, the intern did the job, it must have been his first. He was as jittery as I was, and it didn't go well. I was afraid, it hurt, I could feel the catheter going into my heart, I screamed so loud they had to go and get a senior physician, the intern was drenched in sweat.

In the recovery room where they'd left me, even though I hadn't been anesthetized, I didn't have a call button, and I badly needed to piss.

I was alone, all the staff had vanished, probably caught up in some "emergency" elsewhere. I could hear people running down corridors in the distance, and doors swinging and slamming violently. Then silence. Did they have another person to torture, a coffee break to take, an important phone call to make?

I called out for a long time. No one. I shouted my lungs out, what was left of them anyway, thinking this was only the beginning of my ordeal, since I'd been spared up to now. In one hour, I lost the absolute trust I'd placed in Hospitals and Medicine. Not because of the pain, just because of my need to piss, my boundless fear, the missing buzzer, and the crushing solitude that had gripped me by the throat, in that fucking recovery room for patients who aren't anesthetized before they're damaged.

I was shouting, too, because I was thinking about my father, who had let me down like a bastard, just when I needed him most. I was shouting because I wanted him to see me, there when I was down: wretched, hounded, up shit creek. I'd lost all my arrogance, all my legendary strength. I would have wanted him to be there, by his son who was alone and sick, so he'd feel a little sorry for me, at least, show a little compassion. I knew that for him to show love would have been impossible, he'd never loved anyone but my mother.

Above all, I was shouting because I didn't know how to cry in earnest over my fate.

Ramón came to meet me when I got off the bus, the bandage under my shirt didn't show, I'd told him I'd been for a simple checkup. He didn't bat an eyelid, but he looked at me from under his brows, studied me like a museum piece, I must have looked like a zombie. He wanted to dump me there at the entrance to the farm.

"Okay, kid, I'm going to eat at Álvaro's if the old fool will agree to serve me. It's lamb day and, it has to be said, no one cooks it the way he does. I imagine you have better things to do. We can meet up later, at around three, we have to get some work done, after all . . . Two hours from now, is that okay?"

"Come for a drink, you can go and eat afterwards. Half an hour this way or that won't matter. I need you, Ramón, I need you to stay here with me."

I felt lousy and depressed, I didn't know if I'd be able to make it up the three steps to my front door. The old man stood there for a moment, not moving, staring at me with his eagle eyes, then he followed close behind, pensive.

When I came into the kitchen, I forgot all my anxiety: I did not recognize my house. She had transformed a bachelor's slum into a clean interior, practical and welcoming. Ramón let out a long whistle and gave me a big pat on the back, it hurt like hell, the fuckwit. I had to bite back a cry of pain.

"Well, well, you old pig."

As for her, she was leaning against the sink, waiting. I looked at her: I had to find a way to say thank you, but I didn't know how to speak to women, all the more so when they didn't speak Spanish.

I leaned forward slightly and murmured in her left ear, very quietly:

"*Gracias, señora.*"

I would have liked to say more, but I couldn't, she wouldn't have understood a thing. I merely kissed her as delicately as possible, my dry lips covering hers.

She set the table, she understood we had come back to eat, since I was getting out the ham and the wine. Ramón was by the window, a glass in his hand, going into raptures while he waited.

"Fuck, this country is beautiful, now that we can see it, don't you think? Tomás, you need to trim the fig tree by the door there. It clashes with the inside, now."

"I will."

"It really is a women's thing, cleaning house, isn't it? Unbelievable, they must be born with it in their blood. Or else they have an extra chunk of brain, just for that."

In Spanish, in a trembling voice, she pointed to the table and said:

"You want?"

"Fuck! She can talk, on top of it!"

He was practically spitting with surprise, the old man. So was I, actually, it left me speechless for a few seconds. Riveted.

"She must know how to say, 'Do you want some coffee?',

too. All she has to do is repeat things a little, she's good at remembering."

Like an ass, I felt full of pride.

"So, she must know how to say, 'You want to fuck?'"

Ramón mimed the back-and-forth of intercourse, astride his partner and slapping her buttocks.

I looked at him, stunned. The old man was really letting loose.

"Knock it off and sit down!"

I grumbled, half-angry, half-amused; what a jerk. Ramón went on with his miming, absorbed in his joke, until eventually he sat down at the table.

"Okay, are you finished, or what? Can we eat now?"

All of a sudden, I didn't think it was funny anymore.

He continued murmuring, not the least bit intimidated by my disdain:

"Besides, she doesn't even need to ask, you lucky bastard! All she has to do is wiggle her bum, she has everything she needs right here. Ah, if only I were younger! Holy mother of God, Tomás, if I were your age."

"You were my age once, old fool. What do you have to show for it?"

"I will confess, I wasted my time. But if God had put a woman like that between my legs, boy, I would have taken her, believe me. And I wouldn't have let her go."

"The last time I heard you talking about her, I think you told me she was an illiterate idiot."

"Yeah . . . could be. But who gives a fuck! Kid, who gives a fuck! She expresses herself with her body, and there, man, she's bloody Cervantes! Don Quixote through and through. And not just two volumes, either. She'll give you an entire library. Honestly, Tomás, you know, what do intelligent women do besides break your balls? I wasn't that lucky, I didn't find a woman like this. I'll remain an old bachelor and die alone like a dog. My soul will come back in the form of a crow, like any good, self-respecting Galician, to cry my jealousy to you day and night."

"God forbid, Ramón. I've had enough of your whining for one lifetime!"

It took her only a few minutes to make a salad and an omelet, she had found the tomatoes and eggs in the pantry. We watched her work, like two good little boys with their mommy.

"In the end, I think I'll stay here, boss, if you don't mind. I've had Álvaro's lamb. If Swiss food is anything like the house-keeping, it must be worth its weight in barnacles."

She set heaping plates down before us, beginning with me, and, ridiculously, I felt like a real big shot. After a few minutes Ramón began playing the food critic, chewing deliberately, rolling his eyes from right to left.

"It's not a tortilla, but it's good all the same, don't you think? And tomatoes are good for your intestines, makes a nice change from chorizo. You should open her an account at the grocery, maybe she'll cook typical Swiss things for you? Cheese sorts of things. That's all they eat over there, they melt it with wine and eat it by itself with bread. I saw it on television."

I was listening distractedly, watching Suiza eat. Even when she was eating she aroused me. I was wondering why watching her chew was giving me a hard-on. Surely because of her pale pink lips opening and closing at regular intervals, swelling with the effort. I pictured them on my chest, on my cock. As a result, I got hard as a bull. Weak, half-dead, desperate, and I could still get hard like that. I was still alive, in other words. It almost made me mad to have the old man there, I was desperately hunting for a pretext to get rid of him, but he sat there calmly stuffing his face like nobody's business while he made his remarks.

In an insincere voice, I suggested he go have a smoke outside, and rest in the shade of the palm tree until it was time for coffee. He stared at me with glassy eyes and began chuckling like an old turkey.

"Okay, boss, I'll do that, sure I will. It'll be nice out there in the shade, to get some rest, it's true that now, at my age, I need to rest. You'll bring me the coffee when it's poured, okay? Don't forget I take two sugars, okay?"

I led Suiza into the pantry and fucked her against the wall, my hand over her mouth so that Ramón wouldn't hear her. I was surprised, because it was disconcertingly simple, I didn't hesitate for a second, it felt as if I had seated her on my cock. I couldn't lift her, I was too tired, but all I had to do was bend my thighs slightly, she slipped onto me easily, and it didn't hurt. I remembered Rosetta and the difficulty I had in fucking her quickly, because she was always dry. Here, not only was Suiza supple and moist, and it was easy, but on top of it, it only lasted a few minutes, because of her misty gaze that made me think she really liked it, and above all because she was licking the palm of my hand on her mouth. I couldn't stand it for very long.

Coming back from the fields, I almost felt better from working in the sun with Ramón. Knowing that when I got home she'd be there. The way she walked, hopping slightly, her white skin, her youth, all injected me with a concentrated dose of life. It made me feel as if I were some corrupt old vampire, drinking at the source the strength he needed to live.

She tried, after the evening meal, when I came to bed. In a monotone voice she asked, sort of as if she wanted to buy a kilo of potatoes from me:

"You want fuck?"

I turned my head toward her and looked at her, alarmed. Then I remembered the conversation we'd had at noon, with Ramón: maybe she wasn't as stupid as all that.

Okay, but I would have to tell her. I went closer, put my hand on her lips, repeating, "You want fuck?" and I went "no" with my finger and my head. I wanted to make her understand that you don't ask like that. It's too vulgar, like that, even for a wild beast crossed with a thick brute like me.

I pointed to her eyes, her breasts, her body, and I said:

"For 'You want fuck?' this is how you ask. Not with words."

I put my forefinger on her eyes, breasts, and body, and nodded my head.

Go figure! Impossible. I stood there with my arms dangling, by the bed, wondering how to get through to her, what method to use.

Oddly enough, I don't know how or why, she understood. She sat down on the bed in front of me, where I was standing. She opened her mouth slightly, unbuttoned her blouse just a little, a few buttons between her breasts. With one hand, she pulled her dress up to her thighs, and opened them: she wasn't wearing panties. She leaned back on her elbows and looked at me, her head thrown back a little way, as if I were the only man on the planet.

I flung myself at her like a roughneck soldier, and there I'd been just a few minutes earlier talking about being vulgar, and I said, to myself, "Fuck! You sure know how to ask."

In the night, sitting on the edge of the bed, I watched her sleep, naked and still. What touched me, again and always, was her milky complexion, her seeming fragility. And the absence of hair. Nothing under her arms, nothing on her legs, just a tiny triangle of fine orangey down marking her pubis. I leaned over a little, saw her sex, a delicate shell. I fleetingly recalled Rosetta's, black and bushy, which would suck me into its darkness, a vast thick and curly layer where I couldn't see anything, just a relative moistness, a disquieting void which unsettled me with its mystery. Here, however, beneath the light ginger shadow, I could make out the big pinkish lips and the smaller ones venturing outside, curious but cautious. It was fascinatingly simple, unbearably tender. A shell burst open on the sand. It was all there, palpable and visible. Most often, I wanted to slip my dark, vigorous cock in there, to cleanse it of its bestiality, rinse it with rose, white, and orange. I didn't need to drink to get hard.

It was my insistent stare that woke her up. As soon as she opened her eyes I went deep inside her, I was always afraid I'd come too quickly. My huge hands held her face in place, I locked her gaze in mine, I wanted to be in her head, too, prevent her from fleeing far from me, even in her thoughts.

After I came, I kept her close. She fell asleep again quickly, like a child, her calm breath dying against my chest. I fell asleep, too, but I snored like a lumberjack, particularly as I'd stayed lying on my back, not to wake her.

On waking, I still wanted her. Again. I wanted her little pink sex. Sometimes I felt like I wanted to eat it up. I kissed it, sucked greedily. She would breathe then in fits and starts, feverishly, and beg me about something. There was that floury, sugary smell, that dampness that, ordinarily, frightened me. But it was small and pale, tender and fragile, I felt like the absolute master of it all. With every kiss, every lapping of my tongue she would respond with a wild cry or a cat's growling, a stifled sob or a cascade of laughter. A few seconds, a ridiculous little space-time, and she was no longer there, taut with pleasure. She had come, with unprecedented intensity, and I knew it.

I could never be sure, in the past, whether I'd made a woman come or not. I knew they were experts in the art of deceiving everyone, and I was already sufficiently busy with trying to procure my own pleasure. Why had I never taken the time to look into it further? Why was I so happy I'd made her come? Every time, I would ask myself this, but she never let me interrogate myself on the subject for too long. Invariably, she tugged my head away from between her legs, stroked me until I was erect, slipped quickly under me to impale herself on my cock, to steal from me the fleeting power I'd had over her. I couldn't get away, she was circling my waist with her white thighs so that I would penetrate her as deeply as possible. I was trying to get free, but the moist, silky sheath, her breasts caressing my chest and the avid lips kissing me, all got the better of me, I let her do what she wanted, I was defeated before I even began.

At my first chemotherapy session, once I'd arrived and was sitting in my chair, they offered me a coffee. This surprised me, I thought I was there to go through the mill, whereas coffee, it's kind of festive, coffee . . . Did this mean that, in the end, I was going to have a good time with them? I almost said, "Can I have a smoke, too?"

But deep down, I was so frightened that I nearly passed out the minute they put the drip in the port. The nurses quickly realized that this big solid guy was a touch fragile, they made me lie down on a bed next to an old man who was as yellow and dry as a wax bean and who explained to me that I had nothing to fear. That two years ago, he'd had lung cancer like me, but that it was fine now; no, now it was his bones.

For a few minutes I felt like shouting, "Shut up!" but I just pretended to be asleep so he'd leave me alone.

And there in my bed, with my eyes closed, dead anxious and fearful, on the verge of nausea, I told myself I really was going to die. I looked at the drops of death falling one by one and I wondered which one would be the last, fatal drop. Once the drip was finished, I was pleasantly surprised to find I was still alive. The nurse kindly saw me to the door, saying, "See you next time," with a big friendly smile, as if we were going to meet for an aperitif and have a party.

Ramón drove me home, I felt fine, it was strange. We drank two glasses of Rioja, I had a nap, the afternoon was turning out to be not too bad. I waited. And then in the evening I felt nauseous. It came on like a tidal wave.

During the night, I vaguely watched television to try to forget about all this shit. I couldn't caress Suiza, I felt like barfing all the time. I told her I was sick, I mimed vomiting, she went to bed on her own, after putting an ice-cold washcloth on my forehead. How sweet is that.

Three days, it lasted three days. Nausea to turn my stomach inside out, I didn't feel like doing anything. Ramón did all the work. He'd figured it out. I'm sure he knew. But like always, he didn't say anything. It was better that way. Suiza played the perfect housewife, constantly doing something while making a strange noise. You couldn't really say she was singing, it was more like the purring a castrated cat might make. I could hear her humming all through the house. I didn't feel alone anymore, I liked this constant noise that let me know, better than any radar, where she was at any given moment. A busy little bee, blonde and silky, bringing life into the house.

By Saturday evening I was starting to feel better. The torturer who'd had my head underwater to make me talk had decided to let off the pressure somewhat, to see if I had anything to confess. I was dead afraid that this might be only a passing respite, and that he would decide to dunk my head in the water again so I'd spit out all my secrets and my guts.

By Sunday, I'd come through. No more nausea. I almost felt back to my old self. I wanted to go out a little, see the sun and the fields, the village.

Suiza had been at my house for a while now, and I had totally forgotten about Agustina.

I decided to go up to her place on my way to get cigarettes, since it was Sunday and she wasn't working. I figured I was in for a good telling-off and that it would be legitimate: even if I had only been building my love nest for a short time, that was no reason to neglect her. I approached reluctantly, head hanging, mindful of the storm I was about to weather. It's not that I was afraid, far from it, but I was well aware that she knew me better than I knew myself, she could read my mind like a book and even one of her pertinent conclusions could easily fluster me. I felt so muddled that I was dreading her insight.

She spotted me before I'd seen her myself, and I could hear her shouting from the bottom of the hill, beginning to hurl insults at me. Busy plucking a hen, with a cigarette dangling from the corner of her mouth, she puffed the smoke out through her nose like a locomotive between two invectives.

"Tomás! There you are at last, you scumbag! Have you come to make sure your old nanny didn't kick the bucket? You finally remembered where you came from and who fed you at her breast, son of a bitch?"

She still talked like a fishwife and couldn't finish one sentence without riddling it with swear words or insults. She got it from her father, tall, robust Lourado, the one from Vila do Monte. That was the only language she'd ever learned, along with work, all day long. She was the only daughter in the family, and the eldest. Lourado was mad as hell when she was born, he wanted a son for his farm, not a little minx. His wife made up for it later, she gave him eleven sons. Having kept her end of the bargain, she died not long after the last one, of fulminant hepatitis.

Agustina had taken up the torch, she'd never been to school because of her brothers, and she'd brought them up herself, standing in for their lost mother. Once they were all married off or gone, and the old man had died, she moved in with the Garcia brothers, quarry workers from Lugo, who were looking for a housemaid. Two men instead of twelve felt like vacation. In the village, everyone knew she slept with both of them.

When I was little, I went to play at her place every day,

mainly because of her dog, a horrible yellow pug with big pro-truding eyes that made my childlike self go all soft, because they were always moist. He had a sugary name full of promise: Azúcar. That dog was exceptionally intelligent and I spent hours teaching him complicated tricks, or taking him for walks in a decrepit old baby carriage, where I'd dressed him up like an infant with some old clothes Agustina gave me. I'd often wondered why she had given them to me, because the mere sight of them would fill her eyes with tears and make her sigh despondently. Azúcar played his baby role to perfection: he didn't mind lace bonnets, he lay there on his back with his paws curled over the top of the sheet covering him, and he whimpered whenever I stopped the carriage.

When I had tired of those games or the dog fell asleep, knocked senseless by all the bumps and jolts, I would curl up against Agustina and she put her trembling, perfumed arms around me. Then it seemed that no danger could ever threat-en me, ever reach me. At the time, she gave me a host of little singsongy nicknames, never the same, I was her Andalusian nightingale, her lovely child, her starry stream, her enchanting cricket, and those were the only poetic words in her filthy vocabulary.

I knew the story of the first months of my life thanks to her. On summer evenings when the setting sun colored the fields honey, I would go up to her place and I always found her smoking on the bench outside her door. I would climb onto her lap, she would lift one arm, not to get the smoke in my face, and with the other, after she'd smooth my long black hair, she would give me a tight squeeze. I looked at the plain below slowly drifting off to sleep and I listened to the story of my first hours.

My mother didn't have what it took to feed me, thin and frail as she was. A doe-eyed gypsy, with a slim waist and hair dark as night, twenty years younger than her husband. A real beauty, with breasts like two little plums, not even good for a caress, they were that tiny, according to Agustina. Only her husband liked to suck them. It had taken her three days to give birth to her big baby, who weighed over eight pounds. With the exception of my complexion and the darkness of my hair, I took after my father, Galician and Celtic, and that was too much for her.

At the same time, God recalled the son Agustina was carrying in her womb. He was stillborn because he had no kidneys, poor thing. Perhaps, too, God was punishing her for not knowing which of the two Garcia brothers was the father. Agustina took on the role of wet nurse to relieve her mourning breasts and she spoiled me with the milk of her sadness.

Right from the start, she had felt immense love for me, particularly as I had been the guardrail she clung to for dear life to avoid sinking into depression or even madness. She nursed me for the entire first year of my life, my mother having, against all expectations, given her a free rein by dying from a uterine infection, diagnosed too late, and which had developed into septicemia. Even at the hospital in Santiago the doctors had not been able to save her.

My father was inconsolable and sought refuge in a life of labor, working like a conscript at a labor camp. He neglected me and found it very difficult to love me because he held me responsible, more or less consciously, for the death of his beloved wife. His farm was immense, he'd set it up on his own when he came back from Buenos Aires, where he had made a fortune in the meat industry. It was a huge estate, in contrast with the traditional small farms that resulted from the way land was parceled out in Galicia. When I was very young, he gave me to Agustina to look after as often as possible, only going to fetch me in the evening; when I was older he got rid of me by sending me for a long time to study agronomy, first in Lugo then Madrid. He hanged himself the year I got my degree, feeling he had done his duty, and he left behind him a farm, livestock, land, a bank account filled to overflowing at the Caixa, and a letter. Just a few words where he told his son that, now that he was a man he, his father, was giving himself permission to commit this fatal gesture, and that he was on his way to paradise to be with the wife he had loved so deeply, to give her all the love he wanted, without fear of making children who would send her to her grave.

So, in a way, I was a son to Agustina. She had loved both Garcia brothers, but they been incapable of giving her any more children, with or without kidneys. The elder brother died not long afterwards in a work accident; the younger one two years later from a heart attack, since he drank like a fish and had been smoking since he was twelve. They found him dead at the wheel of his truck: rumor had it he had driven like that for well over a mile before ramming into a chestnut tree.

Now Agustina lived alone, working "under the table" at a grocery store in Lugo. She did the cleaning and would mind the cash register when the boss went for his nap. Her retirement pay was not enough to live on, she'd always worked flat out, but had never paid any contributions to her pension. She took the bus morning and night in her worn black dress and her patent leather shoes that made her ankles look like tree trunks. She didn't want my money. I just managed to feed her a little, by bringing her half a lamb from time to time, or some hunks of beef, vegetables, and fruit. Milk whenever she needed it, she came over and helped herself at the tank, or I'd bring her a little bucket when I came to see her. I gave her the feed for her hens. She had a small trade in capons, and she cared for them like a mother, even singing lullabies to get them to sleep, and people came from far and wide to buy them for their annual festivals.

Although I hadn't informed her, I'd made her heir to half my property, the other half would go to Ramón.

Before I'd even sat down she'd taken out the wine, the olives, and some ham. She cut the bread into big thick slices.

"I'm not too hungry, Agustina."

"Eat, stupid, you're as thin as an anchovy. Your new woman doesn't feed you? The Swiss don't have olive oil or garlic. That's why they're as white as their butts and always sick."

"You already know about the woman . . . "

She gave a raucous burst of laughter, her big bosom shaking.

"Who, in this village, doesn't know, smarty-pants? Paula told me about her, she's the one who found her. As filthy as the pigsty she came out of, hungry as a wolf, thick as two planks. Paula could have called the police, but she's been on bad terms with them ever since they came and got her brother Nicolás for some pathetic story that he'd slapped his wife, that slut from Pontevedra. Paula spent the night at the police station because she was so angry she tried to bite those sons of bitches, and she called them, among other things, 'shit-eaters' and 'micro dicks.' Paula said she would take the girl to the nuns, particularly as she didn't seem too smart, but just then she heard through her cousin Antonio that Álvaro was looking for a waitress. Once she'd cleaned her up she looked young and healthy. It was all arranged and for Paula it was a good deal. Álvaro paid with a lamb and two octopuses, which is way more than the girl was worth, apparently. Anyway, son, if you want to be discreet, don't go kidnapping waitresses in front of everyone! There was a rumor that you'd slit her throat. So, the next day, that asshole Felipe went sniffing around your place, the others put him up to it. He saw her outside your house, alive, so he put everyone's mind to rest. Álvaro's the one who's pissed off. Nobody goes to the bar anymore, apparently he does nothing but complain about everyone. He whines to anyone who will listen that you stole his woman. Yesterday, he even got in a fight with Paolo who told him, between two drinks, that a woman like that was not the right kind of woman for him, and that you did well to take her from him. Álvaro went for his throat, but Paolo, who's twenty years younger and forty pounds heavier, gave him a hiding. The old man is in bed, the bar is closed this morning. On a Sunday! I don't know where they'll all go to get their wine after mass."

She gave me a good look, putting the slice of bread she had just cut down on the table.

"You, on the other hand, where cleanliness is concerned, this Swiss woman suits you."

She came closer to me and sniffed.

"What, he even smells good now? Is she washing your clothes, too?"

She sat down opposite me and looked at me, her eyes half closed, mocking.

"I haven't seen her, but they told me she's as pale as the moon, and has red hair, like a young fox. Stupid enough to eat hay, and fresh like a scallop caught that very morning. You must not be bored, you bastard, judging by the shadows under your eyes."

"She's my woman now."

"So why are you here, son? Not just to tell me you stopped going to the whores? I can tell you need something else besides my blessing."

"That's right, I need you to do something for me."

"Go on."

"Are you going to Lugo, tomorrow?"

"No, not before next Monday. Pedro's son is there at the moment, he came from Alicante with his wife and kids. He's closed the shop for a few days to enjoy having them there."

"You know you could stop working, I could support you."

"You can pay for my coffin, and get your money ready, I want a marble one with golden handles. For the rest, take care of your ass, I don't need charity. And besides, you got family to look after, now . . . "

I changed the subject, sensing the terrain shifting:

"Okay, so you're going to Lugo next Monday?"

"Like I just told you, silly."

"Can you buy me a dictionary? I would've gone myself, but with the work I have at the moment, I don't really have time. And I'm not due to go back to Lugo for three weeks."

"Are you going back to school? All the studying you already did? Nobody would be the least bit surprised if you became a fucking minister in Moncloa instead of being a farmer."

You could probably hear her laughter all the way to the far end of the valley. If I didn't know her so well I might have felt annoyed.

"It's not for me, it's for my woman. A French-Spanish dictionary."

"Why French? She's Swiss isn't she? Why not Swiss-Spanish?"

"The Swiss speak French, Agustina, there's no such thing as Swiss. They can speak German, too, or even Italian."

"They don't have their own language, they have to go stealing from others? The buggers! Then they come and lecture us with their money and their banks, and they don't even have what it takes to talk to each other . . . What a bunch of savages, that's for sure!"

"They do have their own language, Romansh, but not many Swiss people speak it, to be honest."

"Then it's not really a language, is it. Savages, I tell you."

"So, French-Spanish, can you do that? You see, it's so I can speak to her, teach her some words. So she won't be alone all the time, closed in on herself. So she can express herself a little with me and in the village. Say what she thinks or what she wants."

Old Agustina was still looking at me, a little smile in the corner of her lips.

"Of course I understand! You take me for an idiot. You want the girl to speak to you, it's not enough to fuck her."

"No . . . that's not it, it's just so I can understand her a little better."

I grumbled to myself, like a boy who's been caught out, my head lowered over my wine, as I swirled it in the glass.

"If she starts talking, be careful you don't fall in love. You've been without for so long, you're ready to be plucked like a plum. You're not just ripe, you're beginning to rot."

She was inspecting me, with an inquisitorial gaze.

"If you haven't already! All right. Come by next Monday evening, and give me ten euros up front. I'll bring you your dictionary from Lugo. I'll tell you if it costs more than that. Rich as you are, it won't cost you your balls."

I knew she'd find what I wanted, even if she had to go to Lugo on foot to do it. Since the matter was closed, she continued:

"Drink your Rioja, it cost me an arm and a leg, and tell me about the harvest, you're beginning to piss me off, looking all in love, it reminds me that I've gotten old."

Not long after that I started losing my hair. I found a lot on my pillow. One morning, I lost almost all my pubic hair. They hadn't warned me. I got a fright when I went to the bathroom. When I turned around to flush, for a fraction of a second I thought a horrible spider had fallen from my briefs into the toilet bowl, some sort of genetically modified trap-door spider, huge and terrifying. I jumped six feet behind me and crashed into the doorknob.

Where my legs were concerned, on the other hand, I was kind of pleased, they were like an elite cyclist's. I didn't know what I was going to tell Suiza.

The next day, I ran the brush through my hair, starting with my temples. Most of my hair stayed on the brush, and only a few strands resisted here and there, between the hairless zones. So I wouldn't have to go through that every morning, I shaved it all off. It wasn't bad, I had a nice skull. It must be harder for women to have no hair. Suiza was surprised, but she chirped something, and stroked my head gently with a smile that seemed to say she thought it was funny. She wasn't difficult, that girl, I'd done the right thing to bring her home. For the time being, my eyebrows were holding out. My grandfather's nice black eyebrows, the Gabarre trademark. I didn't touch them anymore and I was careful not to stand in a draft. Only Ramón had sensed something was amiss. He just said:

"I didn't know pleurisy made your hair fall out. Well, I caught on a while ago, but you'll have to tell Agustina at some point."

I sensed he wanted to say more, but didn't know how to go about it.

I went to get some wine from Luis, just so I could walk around the village and let everyone see my new look. No one said anything, but in their eyes, I could tell they were surprised. It wasn't so much the hair, it was my face that frightened them: I was yellow as a quince and my cheekbones had rarely seemed so prominent. A regular killer's mug.

Agustina showed up ten minutes later, at full gallop, the gossip radio had worked better than if I'd pasted TOMÁS HAS CANCER all over the walls.

"Hell's bells, Tomás! Why didn't you say something?"

"What did you want me to say, Agustina? I've got cancer, I'm going to die?"

"But people don't always die from it."

"My cancer is a bad one. My chances are slim. I didn't want to worry you, I didn't want to talk about it. The thing is, because of my hair I can't hide it anymore."

"You can't do this to me, my Andalusian nightingale! You can't leave me, I already have too many dead around me. I don't want to be the only one left alive. If you die, I'll kill myself, you know you're like a son to me. The flesh of my breasts, of my milk."

She began crying, and I took her in my arms. I realized that this was the first time I'd ever done that. She was sobbing against my chest, and I kissed her hair, which smelled sweetly of lilacs.

"Agustina? Can I ask you something?"

"Anything you like, my nightingale."

"I'd like to call you Mamá, now and then, instead of Agustina."

She looked at me as if I were about to die in the next fifteen minutes. She went all limp in my arms. I was a bit embarrassed, holding her like that, but I was glad that I'd managed to. I wasn't used to this, I wanted her to know how fond I was of her, the effort I was making to express that simple emotion. I would have liked to tell her that I loved her, but I couldn't, not yet. I was trying to get the message across with my entire body.

She didn't know how to do it, either, she didn't know what to say. She stayed in my arms, this mother full of sorrow for her son. Then she turned back into Agustina-heart-of-stone, to be able to keep going.

"Okay! You do what the doctors tell you, don't mess around. They're all big assholes who just want your money and sometimes they're really bad, so to be on the safe side, I'm going to look after you, too. I'll bring you herbal tea, you have to drink it three times a day. What sort of cancer is it, anyway?"

"Lung."

"That will take special herbs. I'll go pick some this afternoon. Stop by this evening, I'll give them to you fresh, but I'll dry some, too, it works better. You need medals, too. One of the Virgin of Pilar and one of the Virgin of Rocío, might as well not take any chances. Marta is going to Zaragoza to see her son next week, she'll bring back one that's been blessed by the archbishop. For the Rocío, I'll go myself if I have to, there's a bus that leaves from Ourense every month, or I'll ask Alfonso, I think he's going for prostate cancer. The Rocío would be better, all the same, because of your gypsy blood, it will protect you better. I'll go every day and light a candle for you, they'll eventually hear me up there. Don't worry, I'm going to look after you."

"I won't go eating any toads or crushed spiders, Agustina."

"You'll eat them if you have to, even if I have to hold your nose for you to swallow them. Go on, get to work, I have things to do. Stop by this evening, don't forget. And you can call me Mamá, only not too often, because it makes my heart burst with joy, and I'm not very sure, old as it is, how much longer it can hold up."

She left me there, busy with her mission. I figured she'd go hunting for the miracle recipe, spend a fortune on candles, invoke all the saints and God himself to make me better. I even laughed about it, thinking about the earful she'd give them if her strategy failed. I was sure they'd hear her shouting all the way to Rome.

T he following Sunday, when I got back from the fields, Suiza was waiting for me with a basket. She'd filled it with food: chorizo, ham, tomatoes, bread, and wine. A checkered cloth covered part of it. She pointed toward the forest.

"Eat. Sunday."

"I don't have time today. I already let Ramón work a good part of the morning all by himself, we've started the harvest, I have to get back to the fields. I'm running late."

I'd spoken very clearly and loudly, separating each syllable. It's strange how we raise the volume when we think people can't understand us . . . I'm running late: lesson number one, repeat after me. She looked at me with her usual placid gaze.

I started over, even more insistent, arguing:

"Suiza, today is no good. I can't go gallivanting around in the woods, I have too much to do, and picnics, to be honest . . . that's a girl thing, not something for a peasant who's swamped with work and still has the entire country to harvest. The fields are waiting for me, do you understand, Ramón, too. Another time, maybe? I'll eat quick and go back to my wheat."

She didn't move. She was looking at me with her big empty eyes and a faint smile. She hadn't understood a thing.

"Eat."

"No, no picnic . . . "

She pointed again to the woods, and the basket:

"Eat."

Oh, come off it. Okay, no way to get through to her, I took the basket, let's be quick, let's go in the damn woods, let's have the damn Barbie and Ken picnic. Six feet into the woods, no further, we'll have a bite, the quicker the better, at three o'clock sharp I'm back on my tractor and everyone is happy.

She was trotting along behind me, I held the basket carefully, particularly because of the wine and glasses that were clinking together and making my heavy step ring out. Once we were in the woods, the eucalyptus trees had an effect, their fragrance and the ambient silence relaxed me. I stopped soon enough all the same, we weren't there to have fun. She seemed surprised, she was probably expecting to go further in, but she didn't understand my desire for profitability. Docile, she spread the cloth and set out the contents of the basket on the al fresco tablecloth. I went straight for the ham, the bread, and the wine. I was chewing, with one eye on my eucalyptus trees, thinking I would have to chop down the oldest ones before long, since they were fully grown, and replace them with younger plants with round leaves, for their fragrance.

She had disappeared. I was eating all alone with my trees.

"Suiza?"

"Peekaboo!"

She was hiding behind a tree. Oh, fuck! I could tell she wanted to play *Beauty and the Beast:* I'll hide behind a tree and boo! I see you . . .

"No, Suiza, I don't have time, I told you. Come eat, please. *Eat*, please."

Nada. She didn't answer, didn't move. I didn't care, all I wanted to do was eat and get out of there. Inside, I was laughing, I bet that if I left her all alone with the trees, in less than two minutes she'd come running after me, dead scared. Girls are always afraid of forests and beasts.

"Peekaboo!"

I didn't answer, I really didn't want to get into her little game.

"Peekaboo!"

She was insisting. I saw her dress fly past me and land at my feet.

Suddenly I wasn't chewing anymore.

Maybe I could reconsider: the weather was supposed to be fine all week, in one hour, give or take, I had time to grab her, fuck her, have a shower, and at four o'clock I'd be at work.

She'd moved from one tree to another, I saw her running with her bad shoes. Bare-bottomed, with just a little T-shirt that showed the two dimples on her lower back. It reminded me of a thing by Borowczyk, with a beast, there too, definitely more my style than Disney.

I stood up, hesitantly. And then I began running after her. Quietly, so she wouldn't hear me. But she was clever, silent, whereas I made everything crack under my feet. She was really good at hiding, I couldn't hear her breathing. It was dead hard to figure out where she was. There were times I could smell her, her faint odor I knew so well. She was sweating slightly, I could sense she was afraid. Excitement and fear mingled in her, like in me.

Bit by bit I began to enjoy the chase, I was getting more discreet, sneakier. I walked bent over, making successive leaps, tense and nervous. Initially I felt the need to remove my shirt because I was too hot, but then I took off all my clothes, one after the other, to be at one with nature. I just kept my briefs on, because I already had a hard-on and it got in the way when I ran. If I'd had some paint, I would have decorated my body like Sylvester Stallone. I was no longer in my forest in Galicia, I was tramping through the Vietnamese mangrove, stalking my prey. I couldn't find her. I walked, listening out to a deafening silence. Where was she, that woman I was tracking like a hunter? I imagined her trembling, looking at me through the sparse foliage. Where had she learned to hide like this? She had vanished. It was crazy. I called out, "Suiza?" No one.

I had the sudden idea to give out a guttural cry, to frighten her even more and flush her out of her hiding place. She burst out of a bush four yards away. I could have caught her in two strides, but I let her run ahead of me so I could make the most of her tight little sleeveless T-shirt, her bare buttocks bouncing gaily, her firm slender legs in white socks dirty with dried earth. She had lost her shoes long before.

I produced terrifying cries, and every time I bellowed, she would speed up a little and scream, too, higher and shorter, surely in fright. I made detours, I went to her left, to her right, lowing like a deaf man. I was twelve years old, who cared about the harvest, I was running my lungs out, flat out, mindless of the obstacles between us, the branches scratching my chest. I let her get ahead of me, I didn't want to catch her too soon. Too easy. I wanted to play a little.

All of a sudden, I couldn't see her anymore. And yet I was getting better and better at stalking her, nothing cracking under my weight. I shouted again. She didn't jump out in front of me. The bitch! She was getting better at this too. All that was left was her smell, that was where I could get her. I could smell her. I walked soundlessly, sniffing, my movements relaxed, supple and careful. I would never have thought I could be so agile; self-conscious, I'd always thought I was too heavy.

There she was.

Hiding against a tree. I saw her chest rising and falling quickly, her eyes searching the undergrowth, she was crouching, tense, ready to spring. Here I am, my beauty. I leapt forward, caught her by the ankle, since she had instinctively begun to flee before she was aware of my presence, my breathing. She went sprawling into the dead leaves, I tugged her, slid her toward me. I had to let her go for a few seconds to pull down my briefs, she managed to roll onto her side and get away, I was stunned. She ran, her hair full of bits of dead leaves, her T-shirt and buttocks tinged with ochre. This time, I'd had enough, I let out a last war cry and caught her in two strides, she fell face down, she had no more strength. I pinned her down in that position, I took her like that, roughly, since I had won, since I had cornered her at last. I forgot about the eucalyptus trees, all I could see now were her round, earthy buttocks, the little T-shirt riding up with every thrust to reveal her white back, the long groove between her shoulder blades. I kept her in place with one shoulder and thigh, to enter her more deeply and make her accept my victory.

A sudden urge came over me to subjugate her even more, to sodomize her. I slipped my cock between her buttocks and waited a moment, to warn her, so she would understand what I had in mind, so she could say no, since it was so easy to say, even in Spanish. But she was waiting, too, she had stopped breathing, she was afraid, but she didn't say no. My damp cock was beating against her anus, but even wet with her, penetration was difficult. She screamed in pain, but I continued, I wanted to hurt her, so she would understand who I was, for Christ's sake, so she would know I was the strongest, for a while yet, a fleeting time, she was mine, I was doing what I wanted with her, and because I was going to die, I had to do everything I had not dared to do or simply not been able to do. I came quickly, above all because she was granting me her submission and her pain, and her cries awoke in me a suppressed violence that I could now allow to flow freely.

Once I got my wits about me again I held her in my arms, I caressed her hair and asked her to forgive me: I realized suddenly that I was ashamed of what I had just imposed on her, but, paradoxically, still rather proud of myself in spite of everything.

Having this power over her made me a man again, robust

and vigorous, whereas for weeks now my experience of myself had been that of a disease-riddled wreck.

Not looking at me, she said:

"I want all you want."

On top of it, she was giving me her blessing.

The time it took to find our clothes, the picnic, and take a shower, it was five o'clock when I got to the field.

Ramón was driving the combine harvester, Alberto was following with the tractor and the trailer. I offered to take over for Ramón so we could start rotating the trailers again.

"Since you weren't here, I got started . . . With the price you're paying to rent the harvester from the Cooperative, it's a pity to waste time. Alberto was free to give a hand, his company has stopped work now, with the crisis they'll probably go out of business."

Ramón was shouting in my ear, the thresher on the harvester was deafening.

"You should have come and got me, I lost track of time."

What a lame excuse!

"Oh, but I did come! I saw the house was deserted. I thought you went to eat at Agustina's or even into Lugo, maybe. I won't hide that it surprised me, coming from you: to go off enjoying yourself in the middle of the harvest . . . I called out, but there was no one."

He led me away from the harvester and leaned closer to speak quietly in a confidential tone, a concerned expression on his face:

"I thought I ought to let you know, too: while I was looking for you at the farm, I heard a wild boar in the woods behind the house. We should get a hunting party together, it must be enormous, and in heat, given the noise it was making. You'd better be careful, he's got the female with him, I heard her, too, that'll make him jittery and dangerous. He must be at least . . . as big as you, can you imagine? Black as night, and full of vigor!"

"Go on. Have a laugh . . . "

He gave such a broad smile that I could see all his teeth and most of his gums, the old jerk.

When I got home that day, with my dictionary, she had a surprise for me, too: it was Christmas. She'd brought out a white tablecloth, and big candles everywhere, tapers she must have pinched from the church. She'd gotten out the finest dishes, I recognized a few plates Rosetta used to save for Sundays. There was something simmering on the stove and an apple pie. Bread in a basket, red rose petals for a table runner. She must have pinched them from somewhere, too, I didn't have any red roses. She was perfectly capable of taking them from the cemetery, the little bitch. Next to each plate there was a little bouquet of wildflowers, that wasn't as serious: the fields all belonged to me. She had even folded the napkins into convoluted fans, like in some fancy restaurant. She stood waiting by the dresser, with the expression of an eight-year-old kid who's just recited her Father's Day poem. I'd better look happy.

"Gracias, señora."

This always made an impression on her, I knew from the way her eyes smiled faintly, the pale pink color that came to her cheeks, and the particular expression that always worried me she might start blubbering.

I sat down and talked for a long time as if she could understand. I gave her the gift-wrapped package and a big marker. I pointed to the package and said "you," she knew it was for her.

It was the little dictionary, French-Spanish/Spanish-French, that Agustina had handed me when she got off the bus: she'd had it gift-wrapped, like jewelry, and I was surprised by her thoughtfulness. It wasn't exactly Agustina's style to be romantic. Which just goes to show, she was learning, too.

Suiza looked at the present without opening it, without saying anything either, as if she hadn't grasped that it was for her. After several long minutes went by, she began turning it over in her hands, carefully, with tears in her eyes, and that made me nervous. I didn't leave her the time to get all sentimental, I was too excited. I took things in hand, we weren't about to spend two hours here, either. Above all, I was afraid she'd think it was a real present—perfume, jewelry, one of those things that make girls dream. I took the package and opened it, tearing the paper off, still talking. I waved the dictionary in her face, she looked at me, slightly groggy, I knew I wasn't doing things right. But I wanted to look up words for her. She had to understand. She had to show a little intelligence, after all. I began with a simple word: *plate*, and with the big marker I wrote it on the plate that was on the table. I had her read the translation in French. She looked at me, I could sense the anxiety welling up in her, faint yet biting. I pretended not to notice. I wrote on the coffeepot, on the pans, on the table, the windows, the furniture. I wrote everywhere, all the way up to the bedroom, on the sheets, the pillows.

I ended up writing on her breasts, her neck, her thighs, her arms. After that I didn't write anything else because I was too busy kissing everything I'd written on her.

The next morning, I didn't wake up, I was worn out. I emerged around eight o'clock, roused from sleep by the cows mooing, protesting their aching udders. I was in a foul mood, my lungs hurt, and I had a stubborn urge to throw up that kept me from enjoying my coffee. But she had written "sun" on the windowpane, on the spot where it would first appear in the morning when it broke through the mist at last. I forgot my pain and nausea and I left feeling happy, to see to my animals. Ramón had begun without me. Even if he didn't say a word, I could tell that my frequent tardiness was beginning to seriously piss him off, rightfully so. The weather forecast was bad, you could tell it was going to rain, and we didn't have much time to get things done.

After milking, we still managed to do the two fields that were farthest from the village before it began to pour, a right monsoon. We came back to have a drink, Suiza was peeling potatoes, absent and focused on her work.

Ramón lectured me over a glass of wine.

"Don't get me wrong, kid, I have nothing against the fact that you're having a good time, you have a right to, especially with what's going on with you at the moment, but a farmer is a farmer and the livestock and fields don't wait. You're not a real peasant, you have too much gypsy blood, and you went to school, but I know you care about it all the same, you like to see work that's been properly done in a timely fashion, and you love the earth and the woods. I know that all that put together doesn't weigh as much as a woman. And now your hair's all gone. I know it's serious. You don't talk about it, but I'm not stupid, I know that if you go to Lugo as much as you do, it's not to have a good time. I know you've got a season ticket with the assassins, and that you've come down with something vile. I have faith in you, you'll pull through, but you're going to have to let people help you, is all."

"I'll be more careful, I promise."

"Yeah, really . . . "

He was drinking, staring at Suiza's potatoes.

"I'm not telling you this to piss you off, I know damn well that you know what you have to do, that right now it's hard to take care of everything. But maybe you could share out some of the chores . . . "

"Share out?"

"Hire someone, I mean, take on another hand. I'm old, and pretty soon I'll be no use, someone young would help you better. You know I'll keep going on until I reach the end of my wick, because the day I stop working I'll die. But someone young could take over for me, I could show him things as if he were sort of a son and a farmhand at the same time, you see, I could teach him."

"I can't hire some young guy."

"And why not? You think I don't know you're rich? You know, I remember the farm when you had three workers! Your father wasn't as tight-fisted, and yes, he didn't make as much as you. And it certainly wasn't because he was living the life of Riley: other than go to the bar and get drunk, or to the cemetery to cry over your mother, all he did was work."

"No . . . it's not because of the money, it's because of her."

I indicated Suiza with a nod of my chin, I didn't want to risk her understanding.

"Because of her?"

"Can you see me bringing another man here? She wouldn't last two days before he'd try to screw her in the cellar. I don't want to have to play policeman, constantly keeping an eye on things. You're the only one I can trust."

"Can you? I go down to the cellar plenty."

I looked at him, petrified, but then I saw he was teasing me. It was becoming a regular thing these days. He was having a laugh, the old jerk, with all his yellowed teeth bared. I poured him some more wine to calm him down. He took a swallow and looked at me again, in earnest:

"I have thought about it, you know. And I've found *the* solution."

He suddenly hesitated, as if no longer sure of himself.

"But I don't know if you'll like it."

"Try me."

"What about Lope?"

"The half-wit?"

"He's not a half-wit, he's just a bit . . . special, I suppose."

"May I remind you, I've got a farm to run, I'm not trying to start some asylum here, too . . . You know what he's like, he doesn't talk, he mutters all the time. He's got loads of tics. He goes to the hospital in Lugo every month, too."

"That's for his epilepsy. He was born two months before he was due, so apparently that's why. Taken too hot from the oven, so to speak. But he doesn't have fits anymore, he's 'quite stable,' they say, he just goes every three months to the brain doctors' to check on his treatment. I talked it over with him, playing cards last Sunday. He's looking for work. He lost his job at the factory, he was making eyes at the foreman's son."

"Well then there's definitely no risk he'd want to screw my woman, maybe I'm the one who'd have to look out."

And since the old man was already giggling, I added:

"Go ahead and laugh while you have your teeth. You'd have to be careful, too. Aren't you the one who told me the other day that when it came to love there was no age limit?"

"He's not dangerous. And he's not lazy, either: he may be small and thin, but he works like a horse and doesn't drink much. What he does for sex, that's not up to us to judge, there are enough people in the village taking care of that already, and it changes nothing as far as work is concerned. Hire him, you won't be sorry, sometimes he works weekends at Miguel's, and Miguel had nothing but good things to say about him."

I drank some wine, looked at Suiza and her potatoes, her white hands carefully slicing the potatoes into perfectly equal pieces. She was sticking her tongue out, just a little, between her pink lips. I needed her time.

"Tell Lope to stop by next week, we'll see if it's okay."

On the whole, it was a good idea.

After the wine, she took me by the hand and led me out to the old vegetable garden behind the house. It was fallow, except for a small patch she'd scratched at the day before. She pointed to the soil, a square she had turned over, and said:

"I want."

She replaced the stones of the old collapsed wall onto their base and handed me a little piece of paper where she had written, in a fine childish handwriting: repair? I want: flowers, many, vegetables, a few. Cereals? Not know.

I'd done well with the dictionary, I knew she had things to say, urges, desires I could fulfill. I wanted to convince myself she was not completely stupid.

I called Ramón, he liked the idea of doing a little stonework. He liked messing with cement. In his youth, he'd been a mason with his uncle for two years, and he delighted in showing me what he knew. We could spare a little time, a fine drizzle had come calling the last few hours, so we couldn't work the fields anyway.

We started by turning everything over, the earth was very dark and fresh. Ramón had mixed some mortar, we rebuilt the little wall surrounding the vegetable garden, a century-old wall of gray granite. By the end of the afternoon, it was continuous once again, with a few bandages of new stone. Half buried under the rubble and the wild grass I found a little wrought iron door to keep the hens from coming in; Suiza cleaned it and I painted it, and once again it hung dark black on its hinges.

While we were finishing the joints, Suiza set about tidying the unspeakable mess that lay between the barn and the vegetable garden. In her dictionary, she had found throw away/keep. She showed me things, I had to say, "throw away" or "keep," and she made two piles. The first one to throw out, I suppose, and the other to put away.

It didn't take long before it started to piss me off: I had to look up every three seconds to inspect the things she wanted to sort, and all of it was nameless shit that had been rotting there for ages. When things were too big, she came and got me, put her hand in mine, and tugged me gently over to the piece of scrap. Invariably I would say, "throw away," I don't know why she kept coming to get me. When she ended up gashing her finger on an old piece of rusty barbed wire, I lost my temper.

I shouted at the old man to drive her in the Seat to the doctor's for a tetanus shot, I was pretty sure she wouldn't be up-to-date with her injections. While they were gone I jabbed the mechanical shovel into the pile several times over to scoop up all the crap, filled the trailer to the brim, and finally took the whole lot to the dump.

She came back with three stitches and a huge bandage.

I didn't stay angry for long, the old man had me laughing, telling me how clever he had been with my woman in the village: he parked the car a good distance from Don Confreixo's office so they could walk the rest of the way and everyone would see them. And he told me, eyes shining, how the most frustrating thing had been that the tetanus booster shot was given in the arm, because he'd been in the waiting room salivating for half an hour at the mere thought—on the pretext of a medical visit—of seeing my woman's lovely Swiss rear end.

She went to inspect the nice tidy patch next to the barn, and blew me a kiss over Ramón's head with her good hand. I had even gone over it with a rake, to make it neat and tidy.

After a few days, when it had stopped raining, I showed Suiza how to plant, even though it was too late in the season. How to make rows using a gardener's line and cover the little seeds with some earth. Just a little, so they could still see the sower leave. I went back to the fields, I felt lighthearted, I didn't know why. I think it was because she had been talking to herself all morning in her language, while she was planting. It was the first time I heard her say more than three words. Instead of English and German, I should have learned French.

I ran into the priest on my way back from the fields, he was talking to himself, too, his hands behind his back, his cassock flapping in the wind. I had been wondering whether he might turn up because of the candles and the roses.

"Morning, Father."

"Good morning, Tomás. How is the harvest going?"

"I'm none too early. And I worry the rain won't help things. Did you stop by the house?"

"I came to see you, yes. You, and the woman who's living at your place. I saw her, she was in the garden, but I didn't speak to her, I know she doesn't speak Spanish, I would have worried her."

"She's been planting vegetables, it passes the time. But in fact, she wants to grow flowers. She'll bring some to the church, I know she goes there often."

"That's a good idea."

"Did you come about the candles?"

"No, don't worry, I don't care about the candles, I have plenty."

"She wanted to surprise me, a candlelit dinner, one of those women's things, like in the magazines."

"I hear you, Tomás, I hear you. In the future, give her some money, and tell her about the grocery store. That's not why I came. I just wanted to see her, like everyone, I suppose. I hear so much about her, this lost sheep in the wilderness that you went and rescued. I've seen her, and I'm happy for you, she's a lovely woman."

"I feel good with her."

"I can see that, how you've changed. You don't look like a wild man anymore, ready to slit the throat of anyone who doesn't show you respect. I saw your house, too, clean and full of light. That's good, Tomás, I think you're a lucky man and I consider it divine justice that you've been granted some happiness."

"I am a lucky man. I saw right away she was kind of strange, but I know how to understand her now. Her head is not empty the way people say in the village, she's just different."

"Pay no mind to what they say in the village. People love to talk about things they know nothing about. And for your sake, maybe it's better if her head is empty: she won't go giving you tumors over nothing, unlike your first wife, Rosetta. Remember what you've been through already. God loves simple people, it's not a problem."

"So, why the visit, Father?"

"I can see you enjoy living with this woman, that happiness brings out your true nature. But I'm thinking more about her. Have you thought about her?"

"I think about her every day, I don't need to be reminded. I do everything I can so she'll be fine and want to stay with me. Just because I don't go to church doesn't mean I behave like a bastard."

I could feel the anger welling up inside me.

"I'm sure of that, Tomás. That's not what I'm questioning. I can see that you cherish her today as your wife before God. But what do you know of the wearing of time? What will happen if one day you grow weary? If she is as different as we believe she is, you know very well that her fragility will doom her to a life of destitution again if no one takes care of her. And then, Tomás, everyone in the village knows that your health is not great. Your hair loss, your complexion, your cough. Old Agustina comes every day to light candles for you at the church, insulting God, Jesus, and the Holy Virgin. I go to hide in the presbytery the minute I see her, otherwise she'll chase after me into the sacristy."

"I won't grow weary, I will always be there for her."

"And you are sure you will live eternally? Will you be able to overcome your affliction? If you feel something for this woman, give her a status. You know that, without you, she is nothing here. I could talk to you about the value of examples, of faith, of the word of God, but I would rather talk to you about the love you have for her. If you love her, marry her, let her be your wife in the eyes of the world, and may that vow protect her."

"But I've only known her such a short while!"

"Time has nothing to do with it. And what do you risk? Your only fear should be that one day a younger, stronger man might take her from you the way you took her from Álvaro. It is up to you alone to ensure this woman's body will no longer be a conquest, the reward for a victory. Set her free from this false liberty which chains her to the goodwill of a powerful man, possess her even more in the eyes of the world, is what I'm telling you. You know how symbols have the value of the law here. Give her your name, and, paradoxically, you'll be removing some of her chains."

The two of us went on walking, like two crows. The priest small and dry, lively, black in his cassock, and speaking; and me, tall and massive, black from the sun and my origins, lost in thought.

"It's urgent, Tomás. Trust yourself, listen to your heart, it is pure. Think a little about what I have said. You will see that I'm not mistaken and that in my words there is neither Church nor God, just some common sense."

The two of us reached the village, talking about nothing in particular; I carefully avoided bringing Suiza up again.

I stopped off at Luis the grocer's before heading to my chemo.

"Suiza is my wife, now. Everything she buys, you can put on my account. Let her take whatever she likes, don't argue. Everything you sell to her, it's as if you're selling it to me. So, don't you go giving her a wine for tourists, or getting rid of your garbage that's past its sell-by date. Same thing for ham and cheese, you give her the best. I'll come by and pay you every other week, as usual. If there's a problem, you tell me. You don't touch her, you don't question what she says to you, even if it seems complete nonsense. Okay?"

Luis didn't have time to answer, because I was already halfway out the door.

"Oh, yeah! I nearly forgot! Order some candles, you're going to need them."

I was beginning to get used to the chemo and going back and forth to Lugo. The nurses were becoming my pals, they would greet me with a friendly hello, maybe surprised I was still there, coming to appointments. I had my regular chair by the window, I could talk a little about the weather and my fields. I didn't pass out anymore, I drank my coffee.

Between two chemo sessions, I sometimes wondered if I really was sick. There was no sign of the illness. No nodules, no scrofula, no visible wounds. Nothing to display. Just to imagine. Once I got over the traditional nightmares about crabs or horrible beasts hiding in my lungs and devouring me from inside, I stayed by myself with my *nothing*, with the thought that maybe it was all made up, an illusion. A doctor who had given the wrong diagnosis, a simple benign tumor like the one I'd had in my breast. Maybe there was nothing and I wasn't sick. They were trying to cure me of an illness I didn't have.

Seeing myself every morning in the mirror without hair obliged me to admit to myself that I really was sick, and that yes, indeed, it was serious. The cancer had boiled down to this single representation of my bare skull, where the shadows under my green eyes devoured my thin face, my skin drained of color beneath the suntan, and my teeth definitely seemed whiter, with my lips so pale. Unlike the Dalmatian that looks dirty in the snow, I thought my teeth and eyes looked much better than usual, surrounded as they were by the very waxy, Indochinese complexion of my skin.

I would have liked for someone to show me something to hate, something concrete: a creature, an alien, a monster. So I'd know what I was fighting. I had called the laboratory of pathological anatomy to find out if I could have a piece of my tumor, but the horrified lab worker explained that that was impossible, that it had been cut up into fine pieces for analysis. While she was at it she suggested I contact the psychologist in the oncology department, assuring me it would do me a world of good.

Sometimes, I went on the internet to look at pictures, but I couldn't see anything horrible enough to etch it in my memory. So I went on struggling against a colossal nothing, which persisted all the same in terrorizing me.

Everyone in the village had it figured out by now: the loss of my hair signaled my death warrant. They knew I was done for. When people asked me how I was doing, just to be polite, but above all to find out, I answered now, abruptly:

"Not great, I've got cancer."

And then I would watch with delight the effect it had. I loved it. For a few seconds, I was convinced that they thought it was going to jump in their face. They all recoiled slightly, instinctively. Initially they thought it was a joke, then they would examine my yellow complexion, my hairless skull, and they concluded that yes, maybe; and then they wouldn't know which way to look. They mumbled a few words of encouragement.

Finally, what really gave me a thrill about announcing it to them like that was the passing glimpse I saw on their faces of the very fear I myself had felt when I heard my diagnosis. It was disgusting of me, and not just a little sadistic, but I was getting my revenge however I could.

It didn't last long. It was Salva, the vet, who unintentionally taught me some manners. I had stopped off at his place for him to sign some papers for me regarding the inspection of the herds. As usual I was in a hurry, the harvest was taking forever. I turned down his offer of coffee and said, "I'm fine," in answer to his morning greeting, I didn't even have time for cancer anymore. He signed everything quickly, I jumped into the Seat, was about to turn the ignition when he put his hand on my shoulder:

"Take care of yourself, Tomás. You look tired. I wouldn't want something to happen to you, it would make me sad. You're the only one around here who sings flamenco to his cows so they'll produce more milk."

I drove for a while, I felt good. The way he said, *I wouldn't want something to happen to you, it would make me sad* acted like an antidepressant.

I stopped being nasty and waving my cancer in the face of anyone who showed an interest in me.

We finished the harvest on time, even with the two days of rain. I was able to take a bit of a breather. In the afternoon, I took a siesta.

She had written on a piece of paper: *want, see* and then a bit further: *the sea*. In the end that dictionary . . . If tomorrow she wrote *want, see, the moon* I'd be in a real fix.

I asked Ramón about the livestock.

"Just three days."

"You're going on vacation, now? Ah! Women! They'll drive you out of your mind!"

"You ought to find one before you die."

"But I have one, you young virgin!"

"Liar! You would hide something like that from me?"

His satisfied expression, his superior gaze proclaimed his victory. He was drooling with joy, the old man, pleased to see me so surprised.

"Your Nacera, remember? She waits for me now, every Thursday."

I quickly looked away so he wouldn't see my face and the mirth I felt inside. For a fraction of a second I recalled my evenings in Lugo, the bitter taste of them, the quick, lifeless lovemaking. How could I have been satisfied with that?

I couldn't repress a grin when I looked at him again.

Ramón studied me, suspicious, and unmasked me without difficulty.

"I see Milord is biting the hand that feeds him, now that he has Milady at home. But Nacera, you son of a drunkard, is something else, compared to your insipid Swiss woman. Now, she's a woman, a real one! Proper Andalusian, seared by the sun, hard-working, thrifty, and silent. I may even marry her. She makes Galician bouillon like no one else."

"I'll be your witness! But . . . you've been eating with her?"

"Go ahead and laugh, bastard. Whose fault is it? No one to come to Lugo with me anymore now. You know damn well I don't have a license for driving a car. Here it's all right, people know me, but in Lugo? I have to take the bus. I eat, I fuck, and I sleep. I take the first bus back in the morning. She makes me a good price, with wine, dessert, and coffee!"

Eyes shining, he was already thinking about his next evening out. He stepped a bit closer to me and murmured, as if confidentially:

"And I might as well tell you, already twice I didn't pay. She doesn't want me to. I just show up with a few tomatoes, some green beans, and some fresh fish from my cousin Roberto, the one who lives in Ribadeo. For next Thursday, he promised me a lobster and some barnacles. I'm pulling out all the stops for Nacera, it's going to be San Ramón de Vilalba!"

A dazzling smile split his face in two, then he lowered his eyes slightly and fiddled with the handle of his umbrella. He hesitated for a few seconds.

"Okay, I'll tell you: to be honest, we don't fuck every time. It can't be helped, I'm the age I am, and then Nacera . . . Well, you know her, I don't need to spell it out. But in the end, those days are probably the best ones. She cuts my toenails and the hair in my ears, she irons my shirt for me while I drink an Estrella out on the balcony and chat with Xabi the neighbor, the one who's a salesman at Eroski. We eat in front of the television, like husband and wife, and afterwards, at around eleven o'clock, we go for a walk on the ramparts and through town, arm in arm, and we have a drink at a sidewalk café and watch the world and the tourists go by. I sleep like a baby in her jasmine-scented sheets. She may be thirty-five years younger than me, but you know, I think she likes me. You know me, I'm not a mean man, and she knows it: I won't hit her, I don't care about her past or her present as a whore: I make the most of it. I drink just what it takes, and I have some money set aside, since you pay me generously. When I'm there, I pay for a few days' shopping, or an electricity bill, or her rent, it helps her out. All things considered, I'm a good match, what more can she expect?"

"Are you okay with coming on Saturday, Sunday, and Monday? I'll pay you overtime, that means you'll have enough to buy her a little trinket."

"All week if you want, boss."

"Just for the livestock and the hens. The rest can wait."

"Are you teaching me my job, on top of everything? Don't worry, it's like my own home here, and besides, now that it's clean . . . Hey, come and have a drink, we have to celebrate."

"You know I'd better not go to the bar."

"You can come. If it's Álvaro you're worried about, he's not there, he's in the hospital. Diabetes or his legs, or both, I can't remember. It's no surprise, with the amount he eats, the fat pig, it was bound to happen. And besides, he's got another maid now, a Spanish one, he learned his lesson. She's not bad, but she's too skinny. You can see right through her. And then her temper, I can't begin to describe her. Come and see, you can judge for yourself. No one is about to steal her from him, either. Or if they do, they'll bring her back five minutes after they find out they can't fuck her."

In the café, everyone greeted me like in the old days. They figured the woman had been at my place for a while now and I hadn't killed her, so it was basically a fairly banal story.

The new waitress was called Carlota. She had a face like an eagle. Especially her eyes and eyebrows. Big black eyebrows that swooped down toward her eyes in the middle, instead of curving up, and this made her look like she was about to explode. Yellow eyes underneath, like gold. Her black hair framed her brown skin. She had taken care to comb it conscientiously, and had gathered it up in a long, thin, rather flat ponytail that reached all the way down to the middle of her butt.

Álvaro had gone from one extreme to the other, no doubt. To me it was a relief: this waitress had no effect on me. On the contrary, I almost felt like taking to my heels.

As soon as she saw me she delivered a frosty hello and vanished into the kitchen, reappearing a few minutes later holding a plastic bag. She charged over to the table where we were sitting, near the TV screen as usual, and with a sharp, disdainful gesture she tossed the bag down in front of me. It landed with a metallic clang and slid against my arm. She had all but thrown it in my face.

"This belongs to you, I suppose."

Her tone was icy, full of scorn.

I quickly inspected the contents: a faded little dress, two pairs of underpants with rebellious, frayed elastics, some headphones and a few CDs, a worn, scratched CD player, a pink razor, a dried, cracked bar of soap, a half empty bottle of magnolia shampoo. Suiza's meager fortune in a shopping bag from the El Árbol supermarket.

"Yes, this is mine. Thank you very much."

There was no argument. The bag, and the woman it belonged to, were all mine.

I added:

"Two beers, if you please, boss."

I insisted on the word "boss." Her eyebrow quivered above her yellow eye, imperceptibly. She weighed me, gauged me, dissected me with her golden gaze.

It was not a smile signaling the armistice, just a fleeting softening of her lip, a relaxing of her cheek. Peace had been initialed between our two willful dispositions, the borders were where they belonged. We were allies now. She went back to her bar, tall and proud.

As soon as we were alone, Ramón asked me, with one eye on the television and the other on his beer:

"Hey! Tell me! What are we going to do about Lope?"

"Oh, shit! I'd forgotten about him. Listen, ask him to come by on Tuesday, I'll be back. If he agrees to the pay, he can start on the first, it will be easier for the accountant. I'd like a little trial period all the same."

"He'll agree to everything. Where are you going, anyway, to see the sea?"

"To Muxía, the sanctuary of Our Lady of La Barca."

"That rat hole? Why don't you go to A Coruña, the town is more fun, if you want to go out in the evening."

"It's not the town she wants to see, Ramón, it's the sea. And besides, I know Muxía. I used to go there on vacation when I was little, my cousin Mercedes lives there, remember. She'll be able to put me up, she has a bar on the port with her husband, they'll be glad to see me. It will be an opportunity to introduce them to Suiza, she's been at my place for a while already. She's my wife, now."

"That's it! You're right, kid, go get yourself admired and show off your treasure. Puff out your jabot, I'll watch the farm, everything will be fine. I'll see Lope about Tuesday. And bring me back a card from the sanctuary for Nacera. You know what women are like with all those religious trinkets. One that's not too nice, though, all right? Otherwise she'll badger me to take her there."

"I have one more thing to tell you, Ramón, something I've never told you. You're bound to find this a bit strange."

I was hesitating; all of a sudden, I wasn't very sure of myself. I felt short of breath, faintly apprehensive; unless it was shame.

"I love you, Ramón, like a father. I can't imagine life without you there next to me. I should have told you a long time ago."

The old man didn't look up from his glass.

"Are you saying this because you think you're going to die, kid?"

"No, I'm saying it because it's true."

He looked up at me, slowly.

"I know. I've always known. And you know I love you too, like a son. But you did well to tell me, kid. You were right, you have to say it with words."

He put his gnarly hand on mine and we stayed like that for a moment, listening to the silence between us.

I said: the sea. I pointed to the little suitcase where I had packed my razor and a change of clothing. She understood and put her things on top of mine: a dress—the one I'd brought back from Álvaro's; a sweater from the wardrobe, too big and a bit scratchy, but which would keep her warm; a plastic bag for her toiletries.

After milking with Ramón, coffee, and a shower, I put the suitcase in the car. Once I closed the trunk, I couldn't help but give him some instructions.

"If the calf is still sick tomorrow, call the vet, and have him vaccinate the others at the same time."

"Are you going to get the hell out of here, or not? If you want to stay for your animals, just say so, and I'll go with her!"

She was waiting politely by the car. I opened the door for her to get in, and made a little gesture for her to sit down: something that always worked with women, I liked making it. With her it was even better, her eyes filled with tears from the emotion and her upper lip began to tremble. I looked in the rearview mirror for a long time, watching Ramón waving his arms to say goodbye, with his checked handkerchief. I think he was laughing, the old fox, and his cigarette was pointing upward, practically in his eye.

We took the main road, windows open, it was vacation, and I drove with the window rolled down and my arm on the door, like in French movies. She stuck her head out the window, eating midges. She was like a puppy, so happy to be on the road, ears and muzzle in the wind. She began singing her lungs out, some sad thing, and there were times the wind left her breathless. I slowed down so she could go on. It was pretty, exotic, her voice rang high and clear, occasionally off key.

She put her hand on my cock and caressed it. I hesitated for a few seconds then pushed it away, kindly.

I smiled and said:

"The sea, Suiza. We have all of Galicia to go through."

Her expression turned grumpy, fifteen minutes later she fell asleep, her knees in her arms, her head tilted toward me and her mouth half open. She looked like a twelve-year-old kid, tired after a short night's sleep. She had barely slept, I'd heard her banging around the house all night long. She was excited by the thought of a trip, she'd been tidying and washing everything, trying not to make any noise. I think I could have said at that moment that I was the happiest man on earth, if a sharp pain in my chest hadn't come to remind me, at regular intervals, that I wasn't there to have a good time.

I woke her up by the beach just before the sign for Muxía. Very gently, stroking her cheek.

It was the smell that reached her first, for sure. The smell of salt, fish, seaweed, things she wouldn't know much about. She opened her eyes, turned her head, and she saw it. She opened the door, very slowly, got out of the car, her gestures restrained, as if everything would disappear if she moved.

I was sorry I hadn't brought the camera. I would have liked to keep a memory to stick somewhere, even if I knew that she would never forget. She held onto the railing, as if she were afraid she might fall, or be blown away by the sea winds. At the bottom of the steps she reached down to touch the sand, not ready to step on it, and she turned back to look at me, her eyes questioning, she obviously didn't know what this burning white magma was, threatening to slip away under her feet. She stood for a moment staring at the dazzling blue sea, the little town stretched languidly along the beach, the long pier by the port, the hill arresting her gaze. The little white buildings with their roofs pink under the sun. It's true it was quite a sight, all of that. Even I thought the landscape was strikingly beautiful.

Off she went, she walked onto the beach, like a puppy, like a child, she ran toward the water, shouting for joy, almost yelping, from all sides. She went into the water up to her thighs, lifting her dress, she wanted to go farther, but either fear or the cold dissuaded her. She came back to the edge, and then, drawn by the cool transparent water, she dared venture in again. She saw things moving under the surface, she cried out and pointed with her finger at the fish, but they darted by, dark and quick, and she didn't have time to really make them out.

"Suiza!"

I bellowed her name like a deaf man. Everyone on the beach turned around except her. It was impossible to get her away from the limpid blue water. She was already soaked up to her waist and shouting her name from the car wasn't enough. I crossed the beach, took off my shoes and trousers, and in my briefs, I went into the water, too. I went and took her by the hand, she didn't want to come out.

"Come on, Suiza, come. We have to go back to the car now. Come, please."

She left her hand in mine, but her entire body was turned to the sea. I had to arch my back to drag her.

I drove slowly through the port, because she was leaning halfway out the window. She was singing something gentler than before, a sort of lullaby. I'd done the right thing to bring her to the sea, it made her sing. It was still pretty and her voice was pure. I parked the car and we walked for a long time along the shore and through the little port, going back and forth.

Her fascination also had its effect on me, I couldn't get enough of her joy, the beauty of the sea, smooth and clear, the contrast between the crystal blue water and the virginal yellow of the beach, both naked under the July sun. A perfume of vacation drifted through the air, of sun cream and fried food, and the children's cries of joy blended musically with the lamenting of the huge gulls. I felt a terrible pain in my lungs, I sat down for a few minutes on the bench to catch my breath. It was as if my chest were about to tear open. The crab wanted to go back to the sea: that must have been it.

At around four o'clock, I opened the door to the bar, José was behind the counter, with a big smile on his face.

"Tomás!"

"José!"

I gave him a hug, I was glad to see him again.

"How are you? Fuck, what's with the hair?"

"I wanted to change my style. But I'm fine, how are you? The family?"

"Fine! Mercedes is with the children in Ferrol at her mother's, who's sick. You'll see her tomorrow, she's coming back just to see you. I'm still getting used to your hair. Is it a new fashion somewhere?"

I dodged the subject:

"You'll have to forgive me, I couldn't warn you ahead of time, I decided to take this trip sort of at the last minute, on impulse, before the second crop. I wanted to introduce you all to my wife. Her name is Suiza."

"Suiza?"

She wasn't behind me. She was up against the window, looking out at the sea, with her dress still damp and clinging to her thighs.

"Suiza!"

She came over, reluctantly.

"You'll have to forgive her, she's never seen the sea. And on top of it she doesn't speak Spanish. She's a bit strange, in fact. It's because she's Swiss."

You do what you can to make yourself believe.

She had stopped in the middle of the bar and was beginning to slip over to the big picture window again.

"Suiza!"

This time, I shouted. She came back right away. She gave the kind of smile that doesn't want to smile.

"Nice to meet you," said José amiably.

"How do you do. I'm delighted to meet you," answered Suiza, robotically.

José inspected her from head to toe while we were drinking coffee. I didn't like his gaze, it made me think of a shady dealer haggling over a cow at the agricultural meet.

"I'd begun to think you weren't interested in women anymore, Tomás, that you would end your days as a desperate old widower. But I have to admit you've done well for yourself. She's a damn sight sexier than Rosetta ever was, if you don't mind my saying so. She has something . . . I don't know . . . She doesn't leave you indifferent, anyway."

"She's my wife, José."

My frosty tone rang out like a warning, rousing José from his contemplation.

"Right, shall I show you your room? It overlooks the port and the street. It's a bit noisy, but at least Madam will be able to enjoy the view on the sea like the tourists."

Suiza stayed out on the little balcony, her hands on the wrought iron railing, she was still trying to melt into the landscape, to become part of it. I came up behind her, put my arms around her waist to feel her vibrate.

All she said was:

"Gracias, señor."

That evening we gave José a hand at the bar, there were a lot of people, mostly tourists. Pilgrims from the Way of Saint James, prolonging their trip a little further to the sanctuary. It was good for business, José was thinking of enlarging his terrace next year. Particularly since there were buses every day from Fisterra or Santiago now. The tourists arrived in the morning, visited the sanctuary, and left again in the early afternoon or evening, sometimes even the next day.

When there were only a few regulars left, I took Suiza for a little walk along the shore, I didn't want to go as far as the sanctuary, I wanted to keep that for the next day. But the setting sun and the gentle twilight air made me less particular about my plans, and we went along the road as far as Our Lady of La Barca.

It was a church in the sea. A stone vessel.

I knew the place would strike her right in the heart, as it had struck me when I first saw it as an adolescent. It wasn't a love of the past or the air of holiness that had overwhelmed me with beauty, but a sublime alchemy between stone, earth, sky, and water. The colors and textures harmonized in a perfect equation that left you speechless, transfixed by perfection.

She leaned close into me, she needed my warmth, because of the emotion or the evening breeze, suddenly chillier, she was trembling like a leaf. The sea was rough with fire, the stone and sky were splattered with orange. Everything was splashed with the dying reddish color. Even she, ordinarily so white, was the same color as her hair. And then I suddenly understood: her hair wasn't the color of a fox, it was the sun setting on the sea.

Faced with so much beauty, Suiza began to moan, almost inaudibly.

I was leaning against a low wall and I pulled her to me and held her in my arms. I sensed that something was happening that was beyond my control, so I let it happen. I would have had to speak her language. And even then, even if I could speak French, I sensed that wasn't the language she was speaking now. It was the dialect of those who have suffered, of broken, damaged souls. A long expressionless, monotonous lament which had to be allowed to die. I simply rocked her gently, as the sun sank on the horizon, praying that her lament would stop, because I was not sure it could die of its own accord. I realized that I'd always known she had suffered, but now I could measure the full extent of her suffering.

She would only stop moaning late in the night.

I was drifting off as I held her in my arms, leaning against the stones. What roused me from my torpor was the silence. The silence, the chill, and the hard surface of the stone.

I carried her into the church. It was impossible to go any further than the little hall behind the big wooden doors, the grille in between was locked. The red light on the altar scoffed at me in the night, after eight P.M. God did not allow anyone to come near. But the sea breezes could not enter the small space, protected by thick walls. I pushed the heavy wooden doors, without closing them completely, so we could see the moonlight flooding the square outside the church. The sky and the sea were one, now, in a deep blue night. The only way to tell them apart was that, above the horizon, the sky was sparkling with a thousand stars.

She nestled against me. Warm and limp. I opened my leather jacket to hold her even closer to my chest. I sat down on the big worn tiles in the entrance to soak up the night, the silence, the bouquets of stars. The return must be made without rushing her. Successive stages of decompression; bring her slowly back to reality.

I didn't move, I liked the way she was kissing my torso, my belly, I could feel her moving gingerly toward my cock.

I waited.

Deep down I was hoping.

I didn't dare hope. I restrained myself from placing my hands on her head to show her the way. I thought, please, do this for me, fuck, do it for me. Take it in your mouth, go ahead, baby, please, don't be afraid.

I could have forced her all of a sudden, held her firmly by her hair, to make her understand what I wanted, to oblige her, compel her. I put my hands up behind my head, I took hold of the grille, I was afraid of the violence of my desire.

Just the light touch of her lips made me moan. I was finding it hard to breathe, tense with waiting, choking with desire. She took all of me into her mouth, I cried out, it was what I had wanted so badly and she was giving it to me at last. It was almost unbearable, its sweetness too painful.

There was the image of it as well. To see her taking my cock enhanced my virility, and in the dim light I imagined, more than saw her mouth, full of me, a vision that filled me with a terrifying awareness of power.

At the same time, I felt an increasing vulnerability, my reason at the mercy of her lips and tongue. There was something about that simple caress that was degrading and reductive, supremely taboo, beyond normal in spite of everything, and it reinforced my pleasure and split me in two. I hovered between tenderness and barbarity, sharing and solitude, shame and ecstasy. I murmured insults and words of love all at the same time, I knew she could not understand.

My orgasm was a liberation. It annihilated me and broke me, like an enormous, dangerous wave against the shore. I came in her mouth, she didn't pull back, as surprised as I was by such an explosion. She stayed for a moment without moving, then she swallowed. I liked the fact that she drank me and didn't spit me out.

I took her chin in my hand and lifted her head. To wash away my scruples I kissed her gently on her lips, stained with me.

I pulled her back to my heart, inside my jacket. I wanted to say something, to break the silence and solemnity of the moment with an innocuous word, something banal, something insubstantial. She came to my rescue.

"I can ask?"

How crafty of her to ask for something after this! Even the simplest of women are still Machiavellian. I laughed out loud, and complimented her inwardly on her venal nature.

"Anything you like."

"You keep me?"

Shit!... I was thunderstruck. A bolt of shame, guilt, remorse. I had thought she was going to ask me for money, a present, someone's head . . . Who knows what. I sighed softly and caressed her hair for a few minutes.

And spoke, at last.

Suddenly I found the words: my solitude, my happiness at being with her. I told her she had nothing to be afraid of any-more, no reason to suffer, that I would always be there for her, that she could always count on me. I stirred my love with a trowel, I smeared the walls with it, re-papered them from floor to ceiling.

My voice rose in the dark, cold silence, I could see it roll up then slip through the grille and run to the altar to join the divine word. Ah! Inflamed with my own words, I murmured to her about Spain, Galicia, the wind and the night, the pine forests and the eucalyptuses, the stone that never crumbles, my land and my life that I was giving to her. Then I told her about the cancer that was eating my lungs, my fear of dying, and my fierce determination to go on living, if only for her.

Time was passing by and paused there to watch me, sitting on the steps, to see how many seconds, minutes, hours, I would manage to go on spouting my nonsense. I couldn't get enough of it. Listening to myself speak, I thought I sounded good and kindhearted, I went on speaking, on and on, stunned I could let it rise to the surface of my soul, this tortured and ignored adolescent melancholy that had filled me with such unusual energy. I took myself for the spiritual son of García Lorca and Rosalía de Castro.

She'd stopped listening to me for some time already, she was sleeping with her head against my neck, sniffling in her sleep, making the halting sighs of a child who has cried after a big spanking.

She was drooling on my shirt.

Dawn was coming. A pale light flickering on the horizon, the stars fading slightly. She was still sleeping, exhausted from the emotion. I had eventually fallen silent, all my words and feelings dried up. I would have liked to stay there forever, listening to the sound of the backwash pulsating against the rocks and watching the lights of the first boats in the still murky night, setting out for the morning catch.

I carried her, we had to go back, after all, daylight was banishing the shadows. I knew that today I was going to have to remember to say "yes" to her, quite simply.

In the morning, at eleven sharp, Mercedes came back from Ferrol with the children and invaded the space with her turbulent brood.

I had forgotten what a big woman she was, but her vivacity quickly made me admire that outsized body of hers, in a clinging synthetic flowered dress.

She hugged me, elastic and perfumed. Beneath the fat that hid her, there was still her clear, pretty face, cheerful and laughing. And in spite of her weight, she was quick and lively, and constantly in motion. It was almost impossible to keep up

with all her gestures and words. Her children ran all over the
bar, accentuating the impression of a tornado.

"My cousin! Holy Mother of God! I haven't seen you in
ages, but what happened to your hair? My God, it's so weird.
People might think you're sick. What an idea! Are you all
right?"

I knew I mustn't answer, just let her go on.

"I took the first bus I could when José told me you were
coming! Raimonda! Take your brothers and go play outside, I
can't stand the racket! And no going near the water! José!
There are customers waiting! Tomás! Come sit over here so I
can tell you everything. My mother's in the hospital, she had a
stroke. She only has one eye that moves now, poor woman.
What do you expect, with her bad heart and her blood pressure, it was bound to happen. Come on, have a coffee, I
brought some *suspiros* from Bilbao from my cousin Maria,
you've never eaten anything like them. Paradise on your
tongue. José? The coffee? But . . . what's this I see? Who's this
you've brought to see us? A tourist?"

She looked Suiza over from head to toe with a big smile.

"Tomás, you little devil, I can see why you came. It's about
time! Mourning is for women. Where did you find such a
pearl?"

"She's from Switzerland, her name is Suiza. She doesn't
speak Spanish."

I felt like I was reciting my homework.

"In love, the only language that matters is the body's, the
rest you can do without. A woman always knows how to get
across what she wants. You'll find out soon enough."

"I already have, Mercedes."

She looked at me more attentively and eventually came
right out and said, thoughtfully:

"I can see that you have. I can see it in your eyes. Is she with
you all the time?"

"Yes, she lives with me, she's my wife, now."

"And where did you find her?"

"At the bar in the village, she was working as a waitress."

Suiza knew we were talking about her, she waited patiently, slightly to one side. She was studying the wall behind the bar, which was covered in bottles and postcards. She read the labels, tilting her head slightly. Rioja, Ribeira Sacra, Valdeorras, Rías Baixas. She stroked the pictures of the Holy Virgin weeping tears of blood or gold: they had been damaged by the steam from cooking, and faded with cigarette smoke and time.

* * *

Cindy said miracles are crap. I didn't agree, I was sure miracles existed. The Holy Virgin, she got pregnant even though she hadn't slept with anyone. But Cindy always knew everything better than me. Talk about a miracle! Coralie too she got pregnant and she didn't sleep with anyone, it's just that Mickaël ejaculated on her thigh. Besides, maybe the Holy Virgin said she was a virgin because she was so drunk she couldn't remember anything. And anyway, who cares whether she was a virgin or not, she's nice and she's a woman. For once that there's a religion with a woman who's almost more famous than the Good Lord himself, that feels good. But miracles are crap, all the same.

* * *

"We'll have a party tonight, Tomás dear, for once you've come to see your cousin. Ah! I'm so happy you're here. Tell me a little about yourself, you don't look too well. Tell me about the village, who's still there that I might still know? And Agustina? And your farmhand, old Ramón?"

After siesta and a walk on the beach, the evening went by slowly, getting ready for the meal. Mercedes had invited every last relative, close or distant, with a few phone calls. She never missed an opportunity to show off her talents as a chef. She liked to prepare Galician specialties: soups and stews, octopus and shellfish, empanadas. People came from far and wide to eat at her bar. While she was cooking, she never stopped talking, inundating Suiza with advice and words:

"If you come back for Christmas, I'll make you my capon stuffed with oysters: I simmer it very slowly, and baste it often, there's not a better one in all Galicia."

Suiza just murmured "yes," shyly, from time to time, as if she understood, whenever Mercedes stopped to catch her breath. And that was enough to get her going again.

"Before you leave, I'll give you some scallops, too, then you can stuff them for Tomás. I'll give you my recipe: the secret is to add orujo to the white wine, and a pinch of cinnamon with some mild paprika."

With my back against the wall and my legs stretched out on a stool, I dozed, lulled by the culinary litany. I wondered what Suiza might retain of it all. Eyes half-closed, I peeked at her. She wasn't really listening, she only seemed interested in the octopus, which Mercedes was cutting up with great chops of a pair of sharp scissors. The pieces bounced rhythmically onto a big wooden tray.

People began to arrive at about eight, it wasn't dark yet. You could just sense a certain fatigue in the sky, and absolute calm in the port. No more engine noise. Only snatches of conversation rose up to the bedroom, or the clatter of plates and cutlery, or chairs being arranged, their legs scraping the floor. Suiza was asleep against my chest, her mouth slightly open as always, I didn't have the heart to wake her. It was getting noisier downstairs, I knew we had to join them before too many people arrived, so that we could slip in quietly, even if I wasn't holding my breath. I woke Suiza up with a kiss.

"We have to go down."

The men were smoking and chatting in little groups, the woman were chattering, busy around the tables. We landed in the middle of the crowd of cousins and friends, they pulled her away from my encircling arm, the better to see her, feel her, kiss her with resounding kisses, like bursts of machine gun fire.

I let Suiza drink a little white wine, heady, slightly sparkling, oozing with sunlight and the sea. An albariño from Cambados that immediately immersed you in unequalled bliss and beatitude. She had to relax a little, I felt she was nervous, ready to rear up and bolt, like a mare driven mad by horseflies. The wine was a good idea, in no time she went soft and languid, overcome by a delicious torpor. Her gaze drifted into the cigarette smoke, her nostrils quivering, her shoulders back against the chair, her arms dangling along her body, knees apart. Mercedes, walking by, with a gesture that was tactful and precise, took the glass that was about to fall from her hand, and flashed her a smile full of sweetness.

Suiza hadn't noticed: maybe she was still trying to make out the sound of the waves outside, rising in the evening wind in the rare moments of silence between conversations. Impossible. I suppose she must have been cursing us, but she was finding out, at her cost, that Spaniards talk too much and don't listen enough to the sea that has been given to them.

The dinner was a feast; Mercedes, like every great virtuoso, was dancing a complicated choreography with each new dish, weaving her way among the tables, hopping from one guest to another. She was in her element, red and gleaming, spirited and plump, with an eye on everything and everybody.

At dessert, one man pulled out a gaita, another one a violin. And the musicians started in on a *muiñeira*, a very lively, hopping dance that tore into the hubbub of conversation. The younger women cried for joy, pulled back the tables, pushed the chairs against the walls, and began to dance, looking for partners. I quickly went to hide, sitting on the stairs that led to the floors above: I was too afraid a girl might set her sights on me and oblige me to make a spectacle of myself. The only thing that kept me from disappearing altogether was Suiza, I couldn't leave her alone in that innocently dangerous crowd. I was thinking of what would be the best way to get her back, discreetly, so we could slip away.

I hadn't been listening to the music for ten minutes. It was the fixed stare on Mercedes's face that had alarmed me and made me turn my head to see what she was observing so gravely: José was looking at Suiza, his desire like a blade, the trembling of his upper lip uncontrollable. He had been drinking on his own for a while. He wasn't listening to the music anymore, his entire being strained toward her. In his mind, he was already fucking her.

He got up slowly and approached her stealthily. She didn't see him coming, she was out of time, out of the room, absorbed by her sleepiness, lost in her daydreams. I too stood up, and began to move toward her, still a bit hesitant.

José grabbed her arm and yanked her up, shoving her into the middle of the improvised dance floor and out of her lethargy.

"Dance with me!" he ordered loudly, holding her arm firmly.

The music stopped, a few nervous laughs faded into the room.

Everyone turned to look at me.

It was José's obscene hand on Suiza's buttock that propelled me in one bound into the middle of the room. I seized her from my cousin's arms and pulled her back, then shoved her behind me.

"You've had too much to drink. You should go to bed," I said to José.

"I'm dancing, do you mind? Get lost, I have the right to dance."

"My wife doesn't want to dance with you."

"How do you know? Did she tell you? And besides, she's not your wife just because you fuck her, you're not even married. I'm going to fuck her too, I'm sure she'll love it."

I landed a magnificent punch on his face that split his upper lip. He growled, "Fucking asshole, I'm going to split you in two," and came back at me, heavy and powerful. Not drunk enough for that to play in my favor, and he was buff, the fat pig, at least as much as I was. The room had fallen silent, transfixed with fear and surprise; you could have heard an octopus crawling.

I was going to have to kill him before he killed me.

But I hadn't reckoned with Mercedes. She slipped between us before we had time to hurl ourselves at each other. With a fierce gaze, she stopped José in his tracks.

"And maybe *you're* not married?"

A bucket of cold water would not have had a greater effect; those simple words were enough to throw both of us.

He suddenly hesitated, mumbled something unintelligible, in an effort to come up with some pathetic excuse, and eventually he just uttered a pitiful "Mercedes." He had signed his death warrant.

"Twenty years of marriage, four kids, twenty pounds with each pregnancy, and this is all I have to show for it? My husband drunk as a Cossack paralyzing me with shame in front of my entire family and all my friends? José, your miserable life will not be long enough to pay for this. Who do you want to fuck, for a start? Your cousin's wife? When you can't even fuck your own wife? So I have to take my revenge with cake and ice cream because that's the only sweet thing left to put in my mouth? Go on, go to bed, and take your little prick with you. Maybe I should start thinking about looking elsewhere, too, maybe I can find a bigger, harder one, one that actually works: that would be a nice change!"

José did not budge. Mercedes had landed a knockout punch and his eyes were glued to the floor, his hands held before him: the little boy who has just had a good scolding.

I couldn't help but give a mocking a little laugh. A big mistake. Mercedes turned to me.

"You think it's funny? Tomás, I don't remember how old you are exactly, but I'm itching to give you the spanking your mother never gave you."

"Mercedes—"

"Shut up. I'm talking. You don't know? Live twenty years with your Fräulein, give her four kids, then we'll see if you're still laughing, all right? Get your things and take your slut far away from here, she's cute but we've seen enough of her for one day."

Then she turned to the gathering:

"Anybody else think it's funny? Well, laugh away while it's free. Because I'm sure there's not a single guy in here who hasn't been yearning to get into her panties. Married or not. Am I mistaken? And I know a few women who've been cheated on right down to the rind, so they'd better not try and give me any lessons, is that clear?"

I grabbed Suiza firmly by the arm, led her to the stairway at the back of the room, and we hurried up it. In our room, I grabbed the little suitcase and the few things that lay scattered around. Anger made my gestures abrupt and jerky. We went back down, quickly, everyone was still clustered around Mercedes, who was howling like a skunk.

Before leaving, I shot her one last glance above the guests' heads, above the noise and panic, as if in a film in slow motion.

I injected all my sadness into my green eyes, an ocean of regret, and she answered with a look as cold as stone, her face inscrutable. At the last minute, just before I closed the door, she gave me a wink, so quickly that for a few seconds I was unsure I had really seen it.

She was saying goodbye, and that she was still my cousin, in spite of her disappointment as a woman, her lost youth, her children, and the entire litany of petty concessions and great weaknesses that kept her there—whole, alive, cheerful, and stubborn, in spite of defeat.

In the van, we didn't talk.

How could I really be angry with him, that fat lump of a José? But fuck it, I was beside myself, all the same. My anger was in control, the rage was stifling. I felt that close to going back to smash his face in, break his cheekbones with my fists, pummel his ribs, and kick his fat stomach, regardless of Mercedes. I knew that I was feeling the rage above all because I had seen in José the same thing that had overwhelmed me when I saw Suiza for the first time, that insurmountable, bestial desire that could have made me kill someone. What was it she did, to inspire this in every man she crossed paths with? I couldn't spend the short life I had left fighting over her, pissing everywhere I went to mark my territory . . .

I was driving fast, I needed a cigarette to calm down a bit. I made a sudden movement toward the glove compartment. Suiza protected her face with her arm and let out a cry of terror.

I pulled over onto the shoulder and stopped, surprised.

"Suiza?"

I wanted to take her arm but she pushed my hand away, harshly.

I got out of the car without switching off the ignition and walked around to the passenger side to get her. When I opened the door, she began screaming without stopping. I said to her, gently:

"Suiza, it's me. Calm down. Suiza, look at me!"

She was screaming, she didn't hear me.

I said it again more loudly, to drown out the sound of her screaming:

"Suiza, listen to me."

I pulled her out of the car, roughly. I wanted her to stop screaming like a lunatic, I wanted her to hear me. I began shouting, too, suddenly, and shaking her, to make her be quiet:

"Look at me, for God's sake! It's me, Tomás! Suiza, stop screaming, look at me. Do you hear me?"

I led her into the beam of the headlights so that she could see my face and recognize me.

She stopped screaming. In the yellow light, her dress was growing damp between her thighs and urine was running down her legs.

I let go of her, stunned and horrified. Her arms on her head, she was swaying lightly, moaning softly, then she squatted down. She was waiting for the blows to rain down on her.

And so, I guessed something about her. I remembered the little dog my father had brought home the evening of my twelfth birthday, to console me after the death of Azúcar. A mongrel with a white muzzle that I called Golosina. He'd been mistreated, beaten to a pulp by that old drunk, Jesús, and he bared his fangs the minute I went toward him with my Viking sword or a simple kitchen knife. If, while playing, I pushed him against the wall, Golosina collapsed like a pancake and pissed on the floor in terror.

I switched off the engine and went to take her as delicately as possible into my arms, and I said her name over and over, rocking her slightly and stroking her hair. Her hair the color of the setting sun. Little by little she grew calmer. She put her face against my chest and wept, genuinely. I was able to make her sit in the car again, then lay her down by lowering the seat back. I covered her with my jacket and stayed for a long time next to her, sitting on the running board. I lit a cigarette, after I'd opened the glove compartment with extreme caution to take out the pack. I smoked and wondered what I could do, in the warm night, under the starry sky. I wasn't cut out for this, not me. I felt so small, so alone, with my cigarette, my cancer, my rotten car, with this girl, now, who was recovering as best she could from her fit of delirium. She fell asleep all of a sudden, curled up in a ball, exhausted, leaving me alone with my doubt, my questions, my anxiety. Cut off from the little family I had left for who knew how long.

Okay, Tomás, old boy, there was nothing else to do but try to go home, back to the farm and the earth.

I drove, my eyes riveted on the night, hypnotized by the beam of the headlights and the grassy edge of the road, playing the film of the evening over and over in my mind. Mechanically, every five minutes I checked to make sure Suiza was sleeping, and with my right hand I adjusted my jacket, which slipped frequently as we went around the bends.

I had to laugh at myself: for my nighttime driving I had exchanged Ramón stewing in his vomit for Suiza drenched in piss.

When I got home, I put her into a warm bathtub, because her teeth were chattering, then I quickly got undressed and joined her, but just to make things go faster. The bathtub was too small, the water spilled over when I stepped into the tub. I rinsed her off and rubbed her, she submitted, like a prize calf. I held her close, even to dry her off and put her to bed; I was afraid she might fall.

I stood at the window and could just make out the dawn, smudged with big black clouds devouring the dying stars and foretelling rain. The air was fragrant with summer. A few sleepwalking crickets were still singing their love songs.

*

We slept until the middle of the afternoon.

That evening, Ramón told me he'd seen the Seat Inca outside the door, and the farm all quiet, and he'd been worried.

"You see, if you weren't up for the milking, it meant there was something wrong, and I knew you were only supposed to be back two days from now. I took care of the animals, to start with. I have to confess, kid, I was afraid I'd come upon some horror scene in the house, a crime scene. The son of someone who's committed suicide, who's got cancer on top of it, well, he's bound to be a bit fragile. So, like an idiot, I asked every cow, 'What happened? Do you know?' Then to them all I said, 'Did anyone see anything? Tell me, you bunch of jackasses!' I made the milking last, took my time cleaning their udders, I swept the barn, dusted the milk tank, and all the while I kept looking out at the path leading to the house, hoping I'd see you coming. I wanted you to come, even if you were late. But I'd finished everything, there was nothing more I could do. Before I left, I took my courage in both hands and came up to the house, I left my boots and umbrella on the steps at the entrance and in I went. I crept softly over the tiles, like a worm. Put one foot forward, paused, waited a few seconds, then the other foot, ready to turn tail. There was no blood in the kitchen, everything looked normal. When I went past the bathroom, my heart stopped: I put my foot in something that had flowed out into the corridor, some cold liquid that instantly soaked my sock. Jesus Christ, Tomás, I held out a trembling hand to the light switch and the light showed me it was nothing but water, and I had to stop freaking out. I caught myself breathing again, I gulped down all the air I hadn't breathed for the last five minutes. I switched off the light, but I didn't want to, I still had to keep going as far as the bedroom. It took me an age to get to the door."

He began smiling, his good old sweet smile, his eyes lost in his memories.

"You were both asleep, on the sheets. You looked like an egg, you were stuck that close together. And I'll tell you, my Tomás, you're the one who was the white, all around her. I won't hide it from you, it really did something to me to see the pair of you, naked as Adam and Eve. Well . . . you were beautiful, with your differences. I went back to the village to drink my morning coffee at Álvaro's, so's not to wake you, and to watch the news. They have a new anchorwoman with big tits, you have no idea. I walked, I felt all funny with my umbrella on my shoulder, and my brown boots squelching in the mud on the path. My old raincoat was blowing in the gusts, and I knew the rain wasn't far behind. I swear to God I was pleased as punch, son. I thought it was a good thing for you to have a little happiness, now, for the time you have left. Because I wasn't born yesterday, I know very well your days are numbered. And it hurts just to think about it. I would've liked for you to be my son, you know. If I'd had a son like you, I would've had a good life."

He took out his big checked handkerchief, blew his nose noisily in it, and apologized:

"Growing old's no fun, kid. Here I am now whimpering like an old woman. Go on, pour me a glass of Rioja from your own cellar, but a really good one, huh, not an everyday one. That'll set my thoughts straight. Then we'll go and do the evening milking, not every day is a holiday with Sunday the day after."

I had my little card in my hand, and the time for the appointment for my first radiotherapy session. I didn't know where to go, it just said the name of the department and "red strip." I misread, thought that had something to do with the treatment, like "chemotherapy drip," which for a day or two had made me piss red.

The department was underground, directly above the morgue.

I told myself it might be for reasons of practical organization: maybe they had some sort of gigantic dumbwaiter that they used to send you straight down when you were dead, once you'd been radiated and grilled like a chorizo.

I wandered around the corridors and a woman told me to go "that way," waving vaguely. She didn't have time to waste ushering me around.

I found the waiting room, there were three women there already, one young one and two roughly my age. I waited, like a good accommodating patient. Half an hour, three quarters of an hour. Great, I thought, if it's going to be like this every day. I had a farm to run, for fuck's sake, I was beginning to get seriously annoyed when I heard them shout my name. I jumped up from my chair like a puppet and rushed out into the corridor.

"I'm here!"

"What are you doing here? We've been waiting for you!" barked the nurse, fairly irritated. "This is breasts, lungs is over there. Do you have your card? It says on it: red line! You have to follow the red line on the floor."

"Ah!"

I'd have to be careful the next time not to go over to testicles, in case they roasted them with their X-rays.

I waited in my cabin after taking my clothes off, the way the Kapo nurse told me to. I was freezing.

"As soon as the light comes on the above the door, you go out and come down the hall. Get undressed, keep only what is necessary, because of the radiation."

I stripped off completely, to piss her off.

I watched the light, hypnotized, ready to spring the minute the light went green. I was already in first gear, not about to waste time with the clutch. From time to time, I pressed on the accelerator, so I'd be sure to leave everyone behind when the light changed. Light: Go! First!

I ran straight into one of the women from the waiting room, who was bare-chested. She was on her way back down the long corridor from the X-ray room, and with my childishness, I hadn't left her enough time to get back to her cabin. She placed her hands over her breasts and looked down, I hid my privates with my big paws, and mumbled hello, ridiculously. Pathetic. In addition to making me nasty, cancer was making me stupid.

I had a few seconds of radiation, I thought I would feel something, but not even. There was just the "stop breathing," from the microphone, since everyone had vanished and left me alone in Chernobyl. Then a ringing, almost inaudible, almost sweet, which corresponded to the brief moment the radiation entered my body. I went out the way I'd come in. Weird.

Lope arrived that afternoon while I was changing the oil in the tractor: the head of a psychopath on a skinny, stooped body. I almost sent him back the way he'd come, particularly as he couldn't even put two sentences together without stammering, and was constantly shaking with impressive tics, some of which gave me the unpleasant impression that he was making eyes at me.

"No way, have you seen his face?" I murmured to Ramón as soon as he came in. "And even, his face, I could care less, but fuck, doesn't he know how to talk?"

"No, well, yes . . . You frighten him, boss. I swear, give him time, he'll relax. He's a good guy. Buy him a coffee, you'll see, it will be fine."

Annoyed, I invited them to come inside, but I was already thinking the guy would never work out.

In the kitchen Lope went up to Suiza on tiptoe, and instinctively I was about to jump on him, but he simply made a ridiculous little bow then gracefully leaned forward, delicately took her hand, and kissed it, whispering something in French which sounded impeccable, and without stammering. Suiza's eyes filled with tears and she looked at me with trepidation.

"What did you say to her?"

"Just something polite to introduce myself."

"You can speak French?"

"A little, I'm trying to learn. I study on my own with a book and some CDs."

"And just now, what did you say?"

"'Allow me to introduce myself, Lope Blanco Ramírez, at your service, my humble respects, Madame.'"

That half-wit spoke French, maybe only a few words, but in that respect, he was far superior to me. I did not suggest any trial period, I hired him on the spot.

On Sunday, Agustina came by because she had made a tarta de Santiago, "for the young lady to try."

I was no fool, I knew it was all because she wanted to see Suiza, after hearing about her all this time, and to find out whether I was about to die the next day or not.

We stayed in the kitchen for a while, eating and making small talk. As we couldn't find much to say—we avoided the thorny subjects—I eventually switched on the television for the news. I felt a little ill at ease.

Agustina was inspecting Suiza shamelessly, and when Suiza turned away, sensing the inquisitorial gaze on her, Agustina looked me straight in the eye with a cowardly, devious smile, showing me all her missing teeth. That was what was making me feel uncomfortable.

"Have you finished with your song and dance? You can look her in the face, you know, she can stand it. She's used to being stared at like some fairground freak. But you're annoying me, the fuss you're making."

"It's fine for you to talk about looking her in the face, you pig! Besides her tits and her butt, did you notice anything else the first time you saw her? Honestly, what a hypocrite! The gentleman acts the poet, now that he's got what he wants . . . Oh! Peasants, workers, beggars, on your knees! Play the gaita and violin, here comes Tomás, the grand seigneur, the prince of Asturias!"

I focused on my plate. She was right, the old bitch.

Suiza had gone out to hang up the laundry. Maybe on some confused level she knew that we wanted to be alone, to speak like mother and son without her overhearing.

"I have to come here, since you've been hiding her. No kidding, I'm going to inspect her like a hunk of meat at the butcher's."

"I've been meaning to bring her over, Agustina, but I haven't had much time, with the harvest."

"That's no excuse, less than an excuse. Everyone has already seen her but me. Who do you take me for? I told Carmen that you'd invited me over for cod, like a good son, and to meet your new woman. A lie that made my heart bleed."

"We went away for a few days, I took Suiza to Muxía, she wanted to see the sea."

"Did you go to see Mercedes?"

"Of course."

"And how did it go, with your wife?"

" . . . Great, it was great."

I hesitated slightly, and Agustina's perspicacious gaze did not miss it.

"You look like a lion that's eaten a raw carrot. Tell me what happened."

I hesitated for a few seconds. I knew she'd hear eventually—through the grapevine, family gossip—that she'd fry my feet in oil to find out if need be. May as well give in, it was a losing battle, I was no match for Agustina-Gestapo.

"It was José. He'd been drinking. He wanted to dance with Suiza, fuck her in front of everyone. We would have fought like dogs if Mercedes hadn't come between us."

Agustina let out a burst of laughter that shifted the air like a back draft.

"I knew that pig was a pig! Everyone knows it, even Mercedes. He's the only one who hasn't figured it out. Don't make that face, my Tomás, it's no big deal, it will teach him a lesson, the feral dog."

"Except that the way he was looking at her was how I looked, the first time I saw her."

"There's some of that in every man's gaze. That's why we were made with breasts and all the rest, to attract that kind of gaze. In the beginning, that's what brings you together, then later, it's your heart you have to use. For sure you looked at her like that, but now you do things for her."

"Suiza was afraid I was going to hit her, after."

"And who's surprised!" she munched, after taking a last bite from her cake, which she had practically finished on her own. "Women always feel guilty about their sexuality. She must have thought she had something to do with José's desire."

"It took me a while to react, I was listening to Miguel the

gaita player, the one from Dumbría. I don't know what it is about her that drives us all half crazy. I can see she's not like other women, that she gives off this impression of being a little bit stupid and it's not just because of the language barrier. But I don't think she is stupid, not really, it's something else. It's as if she'd been arrested, prevented from growing up. School must not have been much use, she's missing some basic knowledge. But now it's too late, she's got this thing inside her that makes her kind of simple, a little daisy in a field of roses. In the beginning, it frightened me. Now, from taking care of her, it has helped to heal my emptiness, I don't go thinking about my own misery. I feel strong next to her weakness. Look at me: I'm forty years old, could anything better happen to me? I know in the village everyone says she didn't invent hot water, and that my goose is cooked, but I don't care, I can wash in cold water, my hide is tanned enough to stand it."

Agustina gave me an unusually gentle look, full of maternal tenderness, with a soothing smile on her lips.

"Yeah . . . and besides, she already empties out your balls, she's not going to go filling up your head, now is she?"

Agustina would always be Agustina.

"You know what I'm thinking?"

She was suddenly agitated, prey to some intense excitement.

"You should take her to see the Frenchwoman, the one who lives in that isolated house on the road to Friol, that way she could speak her language."

"People say she's crazy, too."

"People say any old thing, you of all people ought to know that. She boils up misery soup, is all. And who isn't a little bit touched by madness? No, I promise you, it's just gossip. That woman could teach your Suiza some Spanish. Words aren't enough, she needs some sentences. The Frenchwoman doesn't speak well, she uses the wrong conjugations, or the wrong pronouns sometimes, but honestly, you can understand her. You could pay her with eggs and milk, some meat, she's not rich, she's like all the old people around here, she'll agree to it. You want me to set it up?"

I rolled a cigarette, giving it some thought.

"It's a good idea, Mamá."

She pretended not to hear, but I could see her chest rise. She went on talking about her plans, she was already drooling over her future arrangements.

On her way out, she simply added:

"I'll go see the Frenchwoman, I'm sure she'll agree. You should be able to go there on Wednesday, son."

The Frenchwoman's name was Francesa: it was easy, a lilting name for this delicate little woman who wore perfume and a lot of makeup. What caught your gaze was her impeccable, bluish-white hairdo, and her very glossy lipstick, as if she'd been eating strawberry jam: it gave her a mouth like an old geisha.

I took Suiza there in the van, explained what I wanted, and she agreed; Agustina had surely already brought her up to date. I told her that Suiza could come for a short visit every day, and that I would come back and get her after milking. I brought her a rabbit, a dozen eggs, and two liters of milk.

"Once she knows the road, she can come on her own, on her bicycle. I'm holding off for a while, because she can't ride very well just yet, I'm teaching her. I don't want her to be out on the road too much."

Francesa pulled over two chairs and invited us to sit down. Then she trained her tranquil blue gaze on me.

"My real name is Ginette, but call me Francesa, like they all do around here, I like it, it's prettier. And with Suiza, it's fine, there's no competition. The next one who moves here had better be Belgian!"

She repeated herself in French afterwards, and Suiza began to smile, too, it must have felt strange for her to suddenly understand everything, not to have to think anymore.

"Would you like some coffee? I have some Lu petit-beurre cookies that my sister sent me from France, I'm rather partial to them. I'm completely fed up with olive oil madeleines."

"Yes, please."

"Why did you come here, Francesa? Did you want to see the sea?" Suiza asked, while Francesa was serving the coffee.

The old woman smiled and translated her question for me.

"I'll tell you all about it, sweetheart, in French, every day you come."

"I'd like to hear, too, Francesa, if you don't mind."

"Ah, my boy! It's my whole story! The sea? Yes, if you like, but not only. The first time was in 1959, can you imagine? My first holiday. My husband was originally from Mondoñedo, but he'd never lived there. His father went to build roads in France, and after three years he sent for his wife. My Carlos was born in Melun. So he was French, basically. But he liked coming back to Spain, on vacation, to keep in touch with his origins. He even thought of settling in Galicia when he retired. He was a welder and I was an apprentice hairdresser. We fancied each other right away. In the beginning, I thought he was Italian. To me he was exotic, with his big black eyes, his tanned skin, and a faint accent that made me melt. I was crazy about him. He knew how to caress me like no one else, in his arms I didn't know who I was anymore. And his smell, my friend! His smell. Narcotic. I would nestle my head against his neck and smell that skin of his, it was made for me, I would go all limp. Carlos was an angel, a gift from heaven. He had gold in his hands. He knew how to fix everything, how to make everything. Whenever anything broke down, or there was a leak, or a problem, all I had to say was, 'Carlos,' and whatever it was was fixed in less time than it takes to say it. Gold in his hands.

It's not something you can learn in school: you either have this gift, or you don't.

"We had two lovely children, Juan and Cécile, twins. Well! I'm not going to sing the happiness tune, but that's what it was. Every year our vacation in Spain, and the children progressing in their studies. The boy was studying to be a pharmacist, and the daughter an engineer. Plenty of work for Carlos and me, the rent not too expensive, in a housing project in Sarcelles, our white Peugeot 404 with red leather seats, and even a little cat, 'Pulpo,' as black as the devil, that we found on the ring road one evening in a torrential downpour.

"There were only Spaniards and Portuguese in our building, we were like one big family, the grass grew right up to the foot of the apartment blocks. In the evening, we would grill sardines in the fields just outside on big makeshift barbecues, and drink chilled wine and talk about life in the old country.

"In addition to his work, Carlos helped out a lot on small building sites, where they paid him cash, under the table, basically, so we lived well, and we were paying off our house in Galicia.

"It was on our way here that it happened. We had decided to spend one last vacation with the four of us together. We knew that later, with our kids' studies getting complicated, it would be difficult to organize, and there would always be someone missing. We were driving at night, it was pouring rain, and this driver had fallen asleep at the wheel of his truck on the National highway and he hit us head-on. There was nothing Carlos could do.

"I woke from my coma three months later, alone, in Bordeaux, in pieces. I had nothing left—no husband, no children. They couldn't even find the cat. Life had taken everything away.

"When I got out of rehabilitation, I continued the journey, what else could I do? I was able to finish paying for the house with the insurance money, and I came to live here, as a tribute to Carlos. I spent a fortune so all three could be in the village cemetery, I go there every day, it's my morning walk. I know that they can see me up there and that they're glad to be here with me. I'll live on our savings until it's time for my retirement, which won't be much, I didn't contribute enough years. But I cut people's hair, now and again, I make do. You see, when it comes to sorrow, I've had my share.

"However, if I can read what's in your wife's eyes, I think she hasn't had an easy time of it, either . . . Well! Shall we get to work? I have to earn my eggs and my rabbit! I bought her a notebook, €1.30 at Luis's, I put it on your account. I have to warn you right away, Tomás: my Spanish is a bit of a mess. Because of my former neighbors, it got mixed with Galician, Catalan, some Portuguese. I haven't had a formal education, in other words. Most of what I know, I learned in bed, if you see what I mean!"

She burst out laughing like a child, before adding with a knowing air:

"And my Carlos certainly taught me a thing or two!"

She stared at the flies on the window, a storm was coming.

"I'll do what I can for her, we'll try to make progress, both of us. I know in the village they say she's as dumb as a goose, but I don't believe that. In the end, it's not a bad thing to be a goose. You see, those birds actually know how to cross the North Sea and half of Europe to get to Spain."

She placed the empty cups on a little tray and said calmly:

"Okay now, my boy, leave your woman with me, we need to get to work, and you must have other things to do, too. I have to tell her in French what I just told you, so she'll know we are alike in some ways, so she'll feel she can trust me. Come and get her after the milking."

That evening, Suiza said to me in Spanish:

"I'm tidy a little then I'm go to bed."

Amazing! It was wild, she immediately seemed much smarter to me.

In the room, it was practically a conversation:

"You say me, Lope, he a prince?"

"No, he's a farm worker. But he likes . . . to speak good French. He's kind of special."

"I know. He's look me not like men. I like him, nice, Ramón is same."

In the morning, she continued:

"The sun is risen, I made coffee. What you want eat at lunch?"

I corrected her, but not too much, because I liked her mistakes, they made poetic phrases, such as:

"It rain tonight, weather is be humble."

I repeated her words, correcting them, rather the way parents do with very small children, so they'll make progress.

"The weather is going to be humid."

But deep down I preferred humble weather.

She wrote sentences in her notebook with the help of the dictionary for more difficult words. She was making progress and, above all, she had a fairly astonishing memory. When I corrected her she almost always remembered and didn't often make the same mistake again.

I was always surprised when she spoke to me, I felt as if I could see into her brain, because now she could say what she felt and I didn't have to guess anymore. It was easier, less worrying. Her accent, too, was enchanting. She would draw out certain syllables and could not roll her "r"s after a "j," or vice versa. She could not say "rojo." In the evening, I often felt like a kid, teasing her about her pronunciation: I would find complicated words for her, full of "j's" and "r's," and make her say them over and over, and I would laugh like a maniac.

"Guadalajara" was a must. She ended up sticking her tongue out at me every time.

What I liked best of all was the "bedroom Spanish" Suiza sometimes murmured to me, and which worked wonders at getting me excited in no time, or at causing me to laugh uncontrollably. Francesa had a dirty mind, with a certain lyrical touch.

I knew her body well, now, but I never tired of it. There were times when our lovemaking was incredibly violent, and other times infinitely gentle. It all depended on what was in her gaze, the way she beckoned to me. I was always amazed by how she managed to play the full scale of her sexuality, which went from first-class bitch to fragile little girl. When it came to sex, there were several Suizas in one, and she knew how to arouse my purely animal side, all drive, violence, and strength, or how to engender a sort of compassion, which compelled me to adoration and tenderness.

She had a particular way of moistening her lips slightly, or of leaving one or two buttons open on her shirt, and then looking at me with total immodesty, a defiant air that made me want to throw myself on her almost instantaneously. Quite often she would come to the barn, pause deliberately in the sunlight, and dance lasciviously around a pitchfork: her lightweight dress made her more naked than naked in the light. But more often than not, I managed to say no. I would shout:

"Dammit, go back to the house! I have work to do. I still have four cows and all the calves to feed."

Vexed, she would turn up the volume. She would come closer, lean into my back or my chest, rub against me like a cat, and go so far as to try and take my cock out of my overalls, particularly if I was carrying milk buckets. Then I would leave everything and give her what she had come for, invariably saying:

"But for Christ's sake, when are you going to let me get some work done?"

Sometimes it was the other Suiza, the fragile one, who climbed onto my lap, put her head on my shoulder and kissed me very gently. The one who rolled up in a ball next to me, all cold after the rain, or frightened after the thunder. The one on summer evenings when the heavens were the color of her hair, the one who said thank you after I gave her a present, the one who liked surprises and nights of partying, the one I rediscovered at last, when we were on our own again after we had been out among people.

Sometimes, too, she simply left it to me. We slept with the window wide open when the weather permitted and, even if the cold or the damp incited me to close it, I never closed the shutters anymore. There were times I would wake from a nightmare or a sudden pain that left me feeling anxious and oppressed in the dim light of the stars. I felt her warm body next to mine, she always snuggled close to me. I reassured her with my body, she was still somewhat fearful she would be attacked. I could sense where her back was, but I always knew exactly where her buttocks were, round and smooth, white and soft. I felt them, I imagined them, I would lift the sheet a little to see them, but it was too dark underneath. So I would touch them a little, to see, the way blind people do. She woke up, she was happy to give them to me, she just pushed her butt toward me and I understood this was for me alone. I knew that I would be owing to her, and that another time it would be for her alone, that I would kiss her in a place that drove her crazy with rapture, and she would shower me with pleasure.

Our bookkeeping was pretty much up to date.

My hair had begun to grow again, a pale black shadow. I was feeling all right. Agustina had given me some sort of herbal tea to drink at night, and I got the impression it was doing me good. I was in a superstitious, voodoo sort of phase. I would stop at every miraculous spring, sprinkle myself with anything that might heal, holy water of Fátima and satanic plants. I lit candles whenever I went by the church, now that I could go there again and my anger was less raw.

I took Suiza and Agustina to Portomarín, for a change of air, to get away from the farm for a while.

Agustina chattered the whole way, fortunately it wasn't very far. We walked along the bridge and through the old streets, we drank café con leche at a sidewalk café. There was only one souvenir shop open and, on the wooden door, there were Aztec figurines made in Taiwan that were supposed to protect you, or bring you luck, or help you pass your exams. While Suiza and Agustina were walking up and down the aisles looking for the best religious trinkets they could find, I read the explanations. There was one little figurine that symbolized health. If you wore it you were protected and healed, all for three euros fifty. In the end, the good old days of indulgences had returned.

I wanted one! I asked Agustina to buy it for me, I didn't want to look like an idiot. The salesman rummaged in his drawer full of earthenware figurines: no more health ones. I went to pieces. This was a sign: I would not be protected, I was going to die, I knew it. He offered us other ones, the jerk: money, happiness, love. In a voice like death, I heard myself saying it didn't matter, I handed Agustina my wallet and got out of there before I collapsed like an overcooked soufflé. I waited in the café across the road for my women to finish shopping for their useless trifles, and I drank two glasses of Rioja to ease the dryness in my mouth and the superstitious anxiety that had been hounding me like a habit ever since I started chemo. Agustina came out before Suiza with a little package wrapped in paper.

"Here, this is for you."

My figurine.

"How did you manage?"

"I told that jerk that you had cancer, and that if he didn't give you that figurine, it would be his fault if you died. So he took a chisel to his door."

I wore it all through the radiation treatment. The radio-therapy didn't burn, except the one day when I forgot to put my figurine around my neck, after my shower. A slight redness, a big square on my chest, like a sunburn. It didn't hurt. When I got back I hurried to the bathroom to hang the figurine around my neck again. Just to see it there, swinging from left to right, made me feel much better. I was no longer alone with my burn. By the following morning the redness has disappeared.

The Aztecs from Taiwan had mysterious powers.

I'd decided to spruce up the farm and throw out anything that was just lying around. I had begun to enjoy comfort, cleanliness, tidiness. Cleaning the area by the vegetable garden with Suiza had made me want to continue, to organize my territory, as if I were dusting off my soul. An enormous spring cleaning, even though we were heading into winter, and because, for

once, I felt like I was in good shape. I even told myself sometimes that I was getting better.

When Ramón arrived with Lope, the old man and the
young one smoking their first cigarettes of the morning and
chatting like two magpies, I distributed their tasks.

"Today, we're just going to make the farm and the immedi-
ate surroundings a bit more presentable: Ramón, you cut anything that is overgrown: grass, brush, brambles. Go around the
buildings, the sheds, the barns. Go all the way up to the path
and burn everything that's dry. Take the brush cutter but be
careful, I haven't used it in years, I don't know if it's still working, I don't want it blowing up in your face. Put on some pro-
tection, too, even if you don't like it. You can trim the trees a
bit, too, same thing, everything that is overgrown, cut it right
down, don't hesitate. Lope, you come with me, we're going to
make some room in the sheds, so we can put away the things
we want to keep. The rest will go in the dumpster. Okay?"

"Yes, boss."

He was already trotting over to the first shed. The perfect
laborer.

"Hey! What about coffee?"

Ramón wasn't buying it.

"Hey, it's time for coffee! 'My Prince!' Coffee first! What
are you getting all excited about now, running away like a
chicken with its head cut off? We have our rituals here, our
laws! Before we start working like Turks, we drink our coffee.
At noon we eat, and in the evening, we have a drink. Come
back here, you son of a moron, come back. Don't go messing
with nearly sixty years of tradition!"

After coffee, we worked like conscripts. I could not stop
myself. Remorselessly, I threw out everything that wasn't indispensable, joyfully burning, sorting, and throwing out some
more. Lope was as feverish as I was, but he lined things up, put
things away, cleaned. He made boxes, boxes for nails, for

screws, for string, boxes for everything. He scrubbed and washed painstakingly, swept and went back over everything after me to polish up. He muttered to himself as usual, but it seemed to me it was something less repetitive, almost more joyful. The volume gradually rose and then all of a sudden, he began singing in a deep, masculine voice, an old Leonard Cohen song that went straight to my heart with happiness. I stood there looking at him, stunned; he had forgotten I was there.

As for Ramón, he was taking it out on nature and saw himself as Attila: he chopped off the tops of shrubs, the arms of bushes, he shaved the hedges, burned the embankments, trimmed the young growth and finished off the old. Wherever he'd been, grass wouldn't grow again. I saw him practically sprinting through the sunshine from one end of the path to the other, using the brush cutter like a weapon. He'd lifted up the protective face mask as if it were a visor, so it served no purpose, and I was sure he had been swearing like the damned until he lifted it up, and that it would end up hurled in rage into the cut grass. He had transformed the prior vague outline of jungle into the gardens of the Alhambra.

That evening, all three of us had our drink outside, feeling the satisfaction of a job well done through and through.

Lope raised his hat to greet Suiza whenever she came out of the kitchen with wine or olives. He always looked at her with a certain consideration I found flattering. Since I had begun to spend a bit more time with him, and had learned to disregard his unbecoming features, his stooped physiognomy, and his constant mumbling, I had discovered a hidden grace about him, a pompous, old-fashioned style, like that of an aging principal dancer, which I chalked up to his sexual proclivities. I could appreciate him. He had managed to win over the old man, too, I could see the gazes of complicity and mutual respect they shot each other. The old man already saw him as a spiritual son, and was showing him all the ropes of the farming trade.

We called him "My Prince," the name Suiza had given him. He was a peculiar character, with the strangest habits, both major and minor: he always drank his coffee in his own cup, which he kept in his pocket, wrapped in a taffeta handkerchief. An exquisite little cup, fit for a marchioness, pink and gold, fairly shallow, with a Moorish couple embracing at the bottom. His nails were polished and very well cared for, very white at the tips, like a French manicure. He wore gloves to work and systematically smeared his hands with cream in an act of totally feminine sensuality that enchanted Ramón and me and drove us to mockery: behind his back we would kiss each other's hand as if we were at some royal court, and curtsy down to the ground, and imitate the frenetic beating of a lady's fan.

His smell preceded him, he always wore a lot of perfume, a fairly pleasant heavy, heady fragrance, which he imported from France at great expense and which was called *Le Mâle*. There too, Ramón and I would guffaw and sputter with laughs of complicity, like two adolescents seeing their first naked woman, but Lope couldn't have cared less. He adopted anything that came from France, because to him, when it came to proper behavior, France epitomized exceptional politeness and refinement. He dreamt of nothing else than to see *Paris et sa tour Eiffel, le quartier Latin et les Folies Bergère*. He never spoke of his homosexual leanings with us, we studiously avoided the subject, by tacit agreement. All I knew was that when he sometimes came to me suddenly to ask for two days off, as if his life depended on it, or he had some ancient relative who was dying and waiting for him to be there before breathing his last, it was simply that he needed to treat himself to two days of sexual debauchery in the Chueca neighborhood in Madrid.

I gave him his days without question, in memory of my own binges in Lugo, and I paid for the bus to Madrid as a sort of incentive bonus. Other than that, he worked like ten men, and I was always surprised by how strong he was for his diminutive size, of which his misshapen aspect gave no indication. The more I watched him in action, the more I knew what made him strange: in spite of his effeminate little habits and his unprepossessing physique, he gave off an impressive sense of power and virility, and a fine intelligence that commanded respect. I liked the guy, and for once I could say it to myself knowingly.

The next day, when I got back from Mondoñedo where I'd gone to see about a secondhand tractor, Álvaro was in the courtyard at the farm. He was inspecting the house, waiting, a cigarette between his lips. He must have been thinking things had really changed here. It was no longer a filthy, desolate dump. You could see Suiza's mark everywhere around the house. The laundry drying on the line, carefully secured with pegs, socks hanging one by one, shirts with their collars downward. The flowers in the borders, the trace of the broom of dried branches outside the landing—regular, rhythmic little signatures. The signatures of a woman. Clean windows, shutters open, smells of laundry. Even the hens were neat and tidy, standing in a row and anxiously staring at Álvaro from behind their fence. Everything was in order, everything was where it should be.

The sound of the Seat engine roused him from his contemplation.

"What the hell are you doing here?" I asked when I jumped out of the car.

"I just came to have a talk."

"I have nothing to say to you."

"I have something to say to you."

I looked at him carefully. I had nothing to fear, he was just an old man, almost thirty years my senior. There was no danger in listening to him.

The old man stared at the house, he knew she was there.

"I want to talk man-to-man, if that's possible."

I hesitated for a few seconds, but finally I agreed.

"Come in."

I knew Suiza was hiding behind the buffet. That was where she always took refuge whenever someone came without warning. Now with Álvaro, she had all the more reason, I was almost sure she would think he had come to take her back.

"You can go out, he's just come to talk to me, we have some business to settle. Go to Agustina's, take her the milk, I'll come for you when I'm finished."

"You come get me, after, or I come when is night?"

"No, I'll come get you. Wait for me, don't worry."

She took some milk and went out, careful not to look at Álvaro. I saw her walking down the path, swinging the buckets lightly.

"She's speaking well, now. You've done a good job teaching her."

"What exactly do you want?"

I wanted to get this over with quickly.

"You see, you see," said Álvaro, scratching his nose, not knowing where to begin. "Don't you have something to drink? It's a long way to get here."

I looked daggers at the old man again, or so I hoped, and it eventually unsettled him. He scratched at the table for a moment with an impeccable fingernail, as if to remove some nonexistent crumb.

"Just one glass, to rinse off the dust from the road," he murmured, lowering his voice further still, until it was almost inaudible.

I went slowly over to the buffet, to have the time to think and try to guess what he wanted from me. I took out a single glass and gave him a generous pour. It would slow him down.

"Forgive me, I'm not being a very good host."

Encouraged, the old man suddenly started up.

"You know I'm sick. Diabetes. My brother already died of it. Before he died, they cut off both his legs, in Madrid, because he got gangrene. And my mother, she—"

"You're not going to read me the entire obituary column, are you?" I interrupted, brusquely, not to have to listen to the whole rotten lineage of the Castro Quinteiros.

"No, no, it's just to say it's serious, that's all. And I have a bad heart. The doctor told me I had to rest, to enjoy myself."

"Didn't he tell you to stop drinking, too?"

I indicated the glass in front of him with a thrust of my chin.

"What about you? Didn't they tell you to stop smoking?" Álvaro protested angrily.

He was right, I was the last one to be giving lessons. I blurted, "Excuse me," before he started up again.

"The doctor told me to stop everything. But they all say that, doctors. You stop everything and that way, after that, dying is a deliverance. Eventually you're the one who ends up calling for the big bitch in the sky. But before I come back as a crow, I'd like to enjoy life a little more."

After that, he quickly raised the glass to his lips and drank it all in one go, then clicked his tongue against his palate. I poured him another glass. He thanked me with a wink.

"It's good, your Rioja, but I came about the woman, as you can imagine."

I clenched my teeth. Álvaro did not fail to see the face I made, and so he instantly added:

"Don't worry, I haven't come to take her back. In any case, she wouldn't want to. Besides, you wouldn't let me, I'm not strong enough to fight you. It's not that she was so bad off, at my place: she could eat when she wanted, she wasn't worked to the bone. I'm not a bad boss. But an old man like me, for a young woman like her, it was . . . not the way it ought to be, it wasn't right. It was good for me because . . . "

He lowered his eyes slightly toward the table, thoughtful, with a faint smile.

"Anyway, this won't come as news to you: where fucking is concerned, women like her, in my life, there haven't been many. Before her, I'd never had any, to tell the truth. I knew how lucky I was. Even if she couldn't cook and was a bit stupid. Now, I have Carlota. She's better at cooking, Carlota, but she's got no ass. No breasts, either, you'll tell me . . . "

The old man seemed lost in his evocation, as if feeling Carlota all over, to see what she actually did have, in the end.

"Anyway, she's flat," he continued, "and so from that point of view, I've lost a lot. But it's okay, because anyway, I'm old and I can tell it's almost over, stuff like that, for me. Before long, only death will make me hard again. With my diabetes and my rotting extremities, Carlota is plenty. It's fine for her, too, life hasn't been good to her, men have caused her too much grief. She doesn't believe in love anymore, because she believed too much. And so, with me, she can relax. I'm the husband and kid she didn't have, the patient she can look after; you see, she would have liked to be a nurse. She can take care of my insulin and monitor my glucose, it gets her all excited, she feels professional. She even does the bandages, Señora Fereira showed her how, the asepsis and all the other crap. The more complicated and disgusting it is, the more she likes it. She knows she's being useful and that I need her. It's a full-time job, it keeps her busy. I give her a little present from time to time—flowers, a pair of earrings, holy images, books on nursing. Next month I'm paying for her to attend a little course at the Red Cross in Lugo to become a first-aid worker."

He paused for moment, took a sip of wine, then continued quickly:

"But still, Suiza was my woman, in a way, before you took her from me. So, you owe me."

"What do you want, exactly?"

"I haven't come here to beg. I have a few hectares of land I got from my mother, over near Miguel's place, Miguel from Pedrouzos, not Silleda. It's not good earth, nothing grows there. Maybe a few potatoes, and even then. Buy it from me for a good price. I can't sell it to anyone who's not from around here, my mother would turn over in her grave and haunt me in my dreams and call me a cursed son. She's probably already rolling from the fact I couldn't get anything to grow! Here, no one wants it and, above all, no one has the money. You're the only one who has any money. You see, if you buy it from me, I'll sell my bar, too. I've got a buyer: Paolo's son, the one who works as a waiter in Oviedo, he wants to take it over to set up a business for himself. He has a little money, he'll take out a loan, the bank has said yes. So, with all that money and Carlota's savings, we'll move to A Coruña, to be near my sister. You know my nephew Santiago, the fat little guy with the glasses? He works in real estate, he says it's a good time to buy, with the crisis the market has fallen. He's found me an apartment not too far from the hospital, for treatment and appointments, and with a view on the sea."

The old man suddenly fell silent and shot me an anxious look.

I was still thinking about his apartment with a view on the sea, I recalled the Tower of Hercules lighthouse and the legend of King Breogán, and the little tram that ran along the waterfront. I stood up and walked around the room, pretending to be thinking, not to say yes right away. I had to look as if I were weighing the pros and cons, so he could think he had obtained a hard-won victory. The deal was more than fair: it was true the land was poor, but I wanted to increase my herd of Galician Blond cattle, and I needed new pastureland. Unless I planted a few eucalyptus trees for paper pulp.

I didn't let him stew for too long.

"Write your price on this piece of paper."

The old man wet the pencil lead with his saliva and went to it: the only hesitancy was in his handwriting, he had given careful consideration to the price.

But then, too, although the price was perfectly reasonable, I took a few minutes before I answered.

"It's a deal. We'll go to the notary's in Lugo. I already have an appointment on Friday, you can come with me, I'll come get you."

I had decided to include Lope as one of my heirs. I wanted the guy to have a safety net, just in case.

I went to get a second glass, and I served two generous pours, to seal our agreement.

"You're an honorable man, Tomás."

Álvaro smiled, he was happy. The matter was concluded. The time for retirement had come. He could already picture himself on his terrace, with the view on the Paseo Maritimo, his newspaper and a drink close at hand. Now he was the one who would go to the café to be waited on like a lord. Carlota would make love to him with her flat buttocks, her soup, and the insulin.

I went back to the village with the old man on my way to get Suiza, so that everyone could sign our pact of nonaggression. We shook hands with everyone we met, in unison and perfect friendship.

Before we parted Álvaro said, staring at the toes of his patent leather shoes and fiddling with his signet ring:

"Regarding the woman, what I said was wrong. She's not stupid, it's just that I didn't take the time and it suited me for her to seem that way. I knew that if I taught her to manage on her own, she would leave."

I left the old man by the entrance to the village, then I went up to Agustina's. From the bottom of the road, I saw Suiza waiting for me outside the door, sitting on the stone steps in the sun. Her head back, her eyes closed, calmly ripening. I felt a wave of love for her, which left me somewhat lost along the way, and I stopped for a moment to swallow my saliva like a happy imbecile, before I could keep going up the hill.

After Agustina's compulsory anchovies, bread, and wine, we walked home, hand in hand. She didn't ask any questions, we both knew the matter was settled.

It was the pain that woke me up at around three o'clock in the morning. A pain in my chest like a dagger stabbing me.

The cancer hadn't forgotten me.

I woke up at nine, the tranquilizers I had taken during the night had tripped me out like a junkie. The pain had disappeared the way it had come, I felt bright as a button and I wondered if it wasn't anxiety, rather, that was stabbing me so often in the middle of the night.

Lope had started with the milking and Ramón joined him before long. It was putting it mildly to say I was ably assisted. The old man knew his stuff, and the young one was following in his footsteps with surprising skill. One hell of a pair. They were adapting marvelously, worked like beasts of burden, and made up for their boss's failings, which were increasingly frequent. I would have to get a hold of myself again, this illness couldn't excuse everything, I had to stop being a drag on others. I left them in the barn and went to see Jorge about the Seat, I needed a new exhaust pipe, you could hear me coming all the way to Santiago. Old Josefina was on her way out of Luis's grocery, I greeted her and slowed my steps when I drew level with her. She returned my greeting and asked for news of Suiza.

"I'll come a little ways with you, I have to move because of my hip."

She walked soundlessly, just her old joints clicking one after the other, as if her entire skeleton was creaking.

"I see her a lot, your wife, at the church, we've become friends. She's made so much progress! She's speaking better and better. You can almost understand what she says. She's kind, she thanks God out loud for being at your place. She thanks God for anything and everything—the rain, the worms, the washing machine that does the trousers so well, the flowers and nightingales. Well, I won't hide the fact that after a while her litany starts to get on my nerves. I told her she could ask for things, too, that she didn't just have to say thank you all the time. She could ask for you to get better, for example, to be cured. Just the main roads, God doesn't have time for side roads."

"The main roads?"

"Yes, love, children, sickness, important things. He's deaf, otherwise. And even then . . . It's better if you don't always make personal requests, but if you show an interest in others, in the world, in war, poverty, all that. It makes you seem selfless, and He prefers that. But to get back to your wife, are you the one teaching her Spanish?"

"No, it's the Frenchwoman who lives on the road to Friol."

"A good woman. Misfortune may have clouded her mind, but she's genuinely a good woman, and she'd be entitled to come and have a word with God and not only say nice things to Him."

"Does Suiza come to the church often?"

"Every day, at the beginning of the afternoon, like me. I'm not that religious, may as well confess, it's just because I'm all alone, and I watch television every morning and every evening, that takes up a lot of time. I go there in the morning, for a break, to chat a little with the old folk I meet on the way. In the afternoon, I go back there for my siesta, I can't have it at home because of my neighbor Felipe, the one from Camariñas: from one o'clock on he likes to saw away at his violin. So I have a conversation with your wife and then I sleep a little on a chair, in the cool. I know that God isn't in there, in that cracked old building, and he doesn't come to our village, he'd only get bored, he's in Santiago or Astorga, it's much prettier. He only comes if you call him, I suppose. I haven't called him in a long time. I have a bone to pick with him. You know, He took my Euserbio from me when the boy was only nineteen. I'll tell you, in private, he didn't fall into the slurry pit, he hanged himself from the apple tree because of some brainless woman in Orense, this girl who was as beautiful as a star, who wanted him and then didn't want him anymore. Twelve hours to bring him into the world, a lifetime to raise him, one minute to make him die on me. I don't eat apples anymore."

"I don't know what to say."

"Don't say anything, Tomás, don't say anything. It's my sorrow, I don't share it. The priest was kind, he's the one who came up with the idea of the slurry pit, so that my son could be buried among people and not dogs. What can I say, he got it from his father, the way he loved women, he had it in his blood."

"Women in his blood?"

"My husband loved them all. I had enough horns to stand in for all the bulls at the Saint-Fermín in Pamplona. But I put up with it, what can you do, when I was young it wasn't like nowadays. Back then you stayed with your husband for life, no matter what he did. Antonio was handsome as Jesus and he knew how to speak to women, but you couldn't count on him. He would say he was coming home at eight o'clock in the evening, but at midnight I'd still be waiting. One day, he went off with a German tourist, this really fat, vulgar blonde who came to spend a few days in the village to visit the region. I got a postcard from Berlin, only once, for our son. He got work as a mason there, he worked on buildings for the government. He never came back, even to finish his own house. I couldn't tell him about his son's death. Don't say anything about the slurry pit, I want to keep going to the cemetery with my head held high. I trust you."

"Josefina, whether it's the apple tree or the slurry pit . . . "

"I know. It does me good to talk about him. He was a good boy. You, too, you're a good boy."

She wiped her left eye with a little white cotton handkerchief, then continued:

"I only have one eye left for weeping, my right eye stays dry, and there is nothing Don Confreixo can do. My eyes are like my children, I still have my daughter, my Lisa. Do you remember her? She's lovely, she's solid, she married a doctor in Santander. An important doctor, a specialist in intestines. My Lisa is a doctor, too, but she does hearts. They cut people up in Santander like steers at the butcher's, they each get their piece. She called her first boy Euserbio, to ease my sorrow. When I see that little boy, all my misery disappears. God making up for things, a little."

"If God really existed, Josefina, maybe people would behave better and the world would be a more peaceful place."

"People are capable of every vice, every compromise, every mistake, and God has nothing to do with it. Because people are fragile. I'm always looking for excuses for the ones who are guilty: you aren't born evil or crazy, you become that way. Look at you, for example, you're just like everyone else, but you've suffered a bit more. There are people who are born to suffer, Tomás, and others for whom life is honey. Maybe in another life things will be sweeter for you. Suffering makes you who you are, like a shrub in the sierra, blown crooked because the wind is so strong. But in your heart, you stand straight and tall, and everyone knows it. You found this Suiza woman, and that's your good fortune. She too is a prickly pear, full of thorns, with a sweet, soft heart. She's as fragile as an egg from the things she's never had, whereas you were given a tortoise shell. She alone knows how to take it off you without tearing your skin, and you alone know how to protect her the way she would like, without breaking her. Put your two fragile selves together and it makes for something solid, a little pair of inseparable souls. It doesn't happen often, but sometimes when you mix two misfortunes well, you can whip up a cream of happiness. And if

God has anything to do with it, that is surely the gift he is giving you. Right, I'll be off, my beans are soaking. See you soon, Tomás, look after yourself."

She left me suddenly in the middle of the street, I stood there, my ears still ringing with the last things she had said, and I watched her for a long time as she wobbled from left to right on her way home.

That evening, I got home earlier than expected, and Suiza was making dinner, humming. It smelled really good: a vegetable gratin, chicken, and fruit salad.

"It's not ready," she said, "still some minutes."

I went up to the attic in the meantime and began to play the guitar, vaguely plucking away, an old Pink Floyd thing, which I'd embellished to my personal taste.

She came up without my noticing, she was watching me without watching me, as if I had just played Beethoven's ninth with an iron hook.

I went to kneel next to her, I had put the instrument to one side a moment before, and she hadn't realized. Her blue eyes came back to me, and she gradually came around. Her lips grazed mine and she murmured, *Gracias, señor.*

All right, it was a major occasion.

"More, will you? Please. More. You know, here is fairyland."

She seemed lost in thought for a few moments then she added:

"You don't move, you listen, you tell me if you know. I find the music for you after."

She told me a complicated story, her Spanish still very sketchy. The main problem was with conjugations, Francesa was useless with that. I could no longer tell who it was about, she, I, we, they, everyone . . .

Her eyes full of enthusiasm, she talked on and on, chirping like a sparrow. I could make neither head nor tail of her story, but I didn't have the heart to tell her. I tried very hard to concentrate: something to do with a woman, running through the desert . . . because she was looking for peace? Maybe . . . She stopped for a break then set off again, worried she would not find peace . . . Blah blah blah . . . She was afraid, she stopped for a break. Some business about a drop of water? In the end, she was exhausted and . . . and calm . . . She saw a something-or-other and hurried under its . . . Branches! She eventually died? But death was a relief? It couldn't be death, she must have used the wrong word. I could not understand a word of her ravings, but visibly she thought it was magic. She stared at me, her eyes wide open and questioning, on the lookout for some sign of approval on my part. I blurted an "Oh, I see!" full of feigned comprehension, which reassured her. She said again, "You don't move," and then she disappeared down the stairs. She came rushing back up with her CD player. She slipped the headphones over my ears and said:

"Here is the story I tell, but in music."

The CD player was ancient, poor quality, it coughed and spit and died of a heart attack before I could make out a single sound. I knew I wouldn't hear a thing, but I waited a few seconds more, to make the most of her big blue eyes, wide with questioning, her mouth open and impatient, her raised eyebrows, her entire face waiting for my reaction.

"I can't hear anything!"

She was about to burst into tears, and I sensed it would be the Guadalquivir at high water, so I quickly suggested:

"Wait a minute, I have an idea. Stay there. I'll see if I can fix it."

I took the gratin out of the oven where it was beginning to burn in earnest and went to listen to the CD in the car: it was *Asturias*. Of course I knew it! Afterwards came a few Spanish guitar classics, dusty old things of no great interest. I went back up, reached for the guitar, and played the damn piece that I'd been stuck with through my entire adolescence. I had sweated blood and tears over it, but for a time, though I was no Albéniz, I had managed fairly well.

She was looking at me as if I were Antonio Banderas or George Clooney: I felt handsome and gifted. There, in my dusty old attic, in front of this woman who had landed here out of the blue, I was the first man on the moon. Due to my emotion, and because I hadn't played it in a long time, I made a fair number of mistakes.

The craziest thing was that I could tell she heard them too.

At the end of the week, when the work was done, we went to the bar for a drink with Lope; Ramón had left earlier, it was "his Sunday" in Lugo, he would only get back the following day. I had to pay my monthly bill at Álvaro's.

When I went in, I heard Paolo squawk:

"Well, lookie here! Hi, faggots!"

I walked right up to him, not thinking, he recoiled slightly and his smile froze.

"Did you say hello? Not sure I heard you . . . "

He hesitated for a few seconds, weighed the risk, compared our builds. He lowered his head. I had the advantage of being fueled by anger, he understood that even if I was weaker, given the cancer, if he tried opening his mouth again to say anything inappropriate, I would tear him apart.

"Hey, Tomás, sorry."

"Hey, Paolo. I think you have some work waiting for you. Maybe you should get back to it."

"You're right, I was about to leave anyway."

He slid along the table and left like a slow worm, limp and shiny.

I waited for him to get the hell out of there, then turned to the bar, as if to say, anyone else want a go?

Álvaro was exultant.

"Tomás, do me a favor, next time, smash his face in, and I'll give you twenty percent off what you owe me."

"Okay! I'll send him flying over the bar, right into the bottles, and make a real strike of it. But I'll give you twenty percent more, for the world of good it will do me just to let off steam."

"I'll pay my round all the same, I'm only too happy to see someone take him to the woodshed, that son of a bitch has ruined my health."

I drank my wine, still fuming. Lope smiled.

"It's even worse when it's true, boss, you know . . . "

"How do you put up with it, why don't you beat him up?"

"It's not that I don't want to, but he's twice as big as me. And if I had to smash the face of every person who calls me a faggot, I'd spend all day and all night at it. I live with it, it bothers me less now than it used to, you get used to everything, even human stupidity. There are not only bad sides. See, boss, you hired me because I'm a fag."

I couldn't deny it. I kept silent.

"So you see, in the end it will have done some good, at least once in my life. But you know, even if I liked women, I can swear to you that I would never have laid a finger on yours."

It was crazy, but I was convinced he was telling the truth. He was one of the best, this guy. As I still hadn't said anything, he added:

"Boss, your wife is really someone special."

"I know."

"Forgive me, boss, but if you know, why don't you pay more attention to her?"

I shot him a sharp look, iridescent with a first twinge of anger: what was the matter with them all, wanting to give me lessons on how to treat Suiza? He looked down, ready for my fist. He was brave, all the same, to confront me like that. On the defensive, I answered:

"I'm the only one who does pay attention, I'll have you

know, the way no one has ever paid attention. What sort of bullshit is this? You think I don't know how lucky I am?"

I was getting all riled up, vexed as could be.

"And besides, what the hell do you know about 'how to pay attention to women'? I thought you weren't into women, anyway!"

It was mean of me. But the more I got carried away, the calmer he remained, waiting for me to stop shouting. At the same time, I remembered his *Lope Blanco Ramírez, at your service, my humble respects, Madame*, and Suiza's eyes full of emotion. So in the end, I stopped.

Stubborn, he dared to speak up again.

"Boss, if you'll allow me, you don't need to fuck women to know them. I was raised by women—my mother, my grandmother, my four sisters, and I assure you, I know them. Your woman, she's like them, they're all alike."

"Oh really? And what is it they all have in common? What is it they want, Mr. Great Expert?"

"Attention."

"Would you stop breaking my balls with this? I show her nothing but attention. I am constantly paying attention to her."

"Then why is she dressed like a slattern?"

I was speechless, stunned.

"Does she have any perfume, beauty products, hand cream, makeup?"

"She doesn't like that stuff, she never uses it."

"To know for sure, she'd have to start by having some. Sometimes I give her my hand cream, and every Thursday I lend her my tweezers."

I didn't know what to say, and he wouldn't leave me alone.

"Do you give her presents?"

And after thinking for a moment:

"They're no different from us, actually, we like presents, too."

"You're pissing me off with all this . . . You piss me off, that's all there is to it. Right, I'm going home, I'm exhausted, see you tomorrow."

Furious, I just left him there like a piece of shit.

Suiza flattened herself against me in the barn, because she'd had a bath, and she wanted me to smell the perfume Luis had given her, a sample, when she bought two shaving creams. Perfume, what a coincidence.

I was in a bad mood, I hadn't slept much, I'd woken at two o'clock in the morning, coughing, a hacking cough that tore out anything I had left in the way of lungs. These were no fits of anxiety. I coughed like the damned, and so I got up, not to wake Suiza, and went to smoke a cigarette in the courtyard, under the stars, because that was the only thing that would calm my nerves. Hair of the dog. I knew I was fucked, but I went on ruining my health so it would go faster. And above all, tobacco calmed me down better than anything, in spite of the fear, in spite of my certainty that it was hastening me to my grave. I knew my path was all laid out, and I wasn't prepared to forego these ephemeral moments of pleasure. In the halo of light from the kitchen, I thought back on the conversation with Lope, and I knew he was right, even though I couldn't completely accept it.

I went back to bed two hours later, and in the morning, I could feel the fatigue wearing me down.

Suiza had no clue how weak I felt, she went on rubbing up against me so I'd give her my opinion about the perfume. I'd have to have a word with Luis, I couldn't believe the stench, just because it was free, that was no excuse. Under her bath towel she was naked, she began doing a ridiculous belly dance, since the so-called alluring perfume had not had any effect.

Her breasts on the verge of brimming over, her pink mouth, and her slim legs restored some of my energy and desire, and I left the livestock—I only had the calves left to feed—to run after her. I caught up with her in the shower, but I slipped on the shower tray full of shampoo. I eventually caught her in the bedroom, between the wardrobe and the window, but I couldn't penetrate her. My erection was not equal to my desire, and this took me by surprise. Even my cock was giving up on me. It remained hopelessly flaccid, I looked at it as if it didn't belong to me. This was the first time this had ever happened with Suiza. She caressed me gently, and murmured:

"Easy, no worry. Later, this evening, tomorrow. No problem."

No problem? Typical woman, yeah sure! I tried to reassure myself: it was the fatigue, the lack of sleep, all I needed was a little rest. I watched her getting dressed in a beam of sun sparkling with dust motes. I soaked up her slow gestures, as she was pulling on her panties, fastening her bra, her gaze lost at the edge of the still-sleeping forest. Suddenly I thought of Lope, and I emerged from my blindness: in a flash of lucidity I saw Rosetta's huge panties and the worn bra, gray with age. The dress that was too big, and which she tightened with the little string. I didn't need to look down, I knew that on her feet I would see a pair of ugly faded pumps which no longer stayed on properly. She smiled at me, turning her head slightly, because she could tell I was looking at her. Lope was right: pay some attention.

I sprang to my feet, I would have left then and there if there hadn't been the livestock to finish. Surprised, she flattened herself against the wall to let me go by. She must have thought I was upset because of some urgent chores and she reverted to her usual placidity.

"What you want eat for lunch?"

"Today, when I'm finished with the livestock, we'll go to town, and we'll eat there, don't make anything."

I took her to Lugo in the Seat. It was the big city, she felt a bit lost. Like me, she had forgotten there were places with so many people, shops, noise. At the bank, I withdrew a lot of money, cash. I was reminded that I was rich because of the obsequious manner of the bank employee, his polite smile stuck on his face and the way he took his time to answer my questions, as if hunting for his words one by one. Sugary as a big piece of Turkish delight, he was sticky with politeness, dripping with pompous small talk. Sometimes, his sidelong glance passed over Suiza, furtively. He was dying to have a closer look at this strange girl, as white as a seagull, clinging to the Neanderthal she was using as a perch, the good client of his provincial little branch office. He walked us to the door, still talking, and for a fraction of a second I wondered if he would follow us out. He watched us walk away, this rough, ill-assorted couple, radiant with the peasant exoticism of another age.

We were in the street. A river of cars awaited us, dangerous and threatening between the asphalt shores steaming in the late morning sun. Fortunately, there was my big hand to hold her, because she was walking unsteadily, as dizzy as I was from the children's cries, the quick conversations she could only catch snatches of, the colorful signs, the shop windows over-flowing with clothes, books, shoes. There were also tempting pastries, smelling sweet and oven-warm, luring us, and dark narrow delicatessens like Aladdin's caves, their walls cascading with ham, their display cases treasure chests of chorizo. It must have been disorientating for someone from Switzerland. We drank café con leche in a bar and it was like being back in the village. The men were watching television and eating sticky pastries, wiping their fingers on little paper napkins they tossed to the floor. What was different here was that no one stared at her and no one, apparently, wanted to screw her right there and then. Except for me and my soft cock.

I took her hand as soon as we went outside, she felt safe with me that way, attached to me in the crowd.

At the Corte Inglés I said:

"Buy what you want, what you need. We'll start with the underwear."

The saleswoman came rushing up to her.

"May I help you, señora?"

"La señora doesn't speak very good Spanish, she's a foreigner. Can you advise her?"

She tried on superb ensembles, in pastel colors or gingham, and even some rather naughty things. It made her more beautiful than when she was naked, more mysterious. Gift-wrapped.

"Try some more, get a few. At least seven, one for each day of the week."

The saleswoman liked me. She even went to get me a coffee. I took advantage of her absence to go into the cabin and caress Suiza, who was wearing a lacy black thing with something-or-other cups, which put her breasts on display as if they were on a platter of fruit. I crushed her against the mirror and I would have gladly fucked her, since now I finally felt in sync with my cock again, but the warder had come back with the coffee and barked a "please, sir!" full of disgust.

"Get some perfume, too. I can't stand the one from Luis's place."

In the luxury perfume department, a saleswoman dressed like an air hostess gave us the sales pitch, waving bottles of Dior and Givenchy under our noses, flasks as shiny as diamonds. I was ready to buy the entire stock, but Suiza didn't want to, she said it smelled of old witches. Witch. I was flabbergasted that she knew the word. But that was what she said, and I understood. Too heavy for her. The saleswoman put on a smug expression, and invited us to go down to the lower level, to the supermarket, since Madam, visibly, preferred the cheaper items. There, Suiza found what she was looking for: lots of jars of face cream and body lotion, a bottle of lilac perfume, and a little makeup. She knew what she wanted, she took a spray thingy in both hands, turned to me and said:

"I can?"

I invariably said yes, in the end she no longer asked. Lope was right. She took things I would have never even thought existed, and which seemed completely ludicrous: cream for "dry feet," deodorant, eyeliner, body lotion. Every time she put something in the shopping cart I looked at it with surprise and mused that the cosmetic industry must have good times ahead. They had thought of everything, those people, there was not a single spot on the body that didn't have its own scrub, ointment, perfume, or tonic. We finished off with razors, toothbrushes, soap, egg shampoo for blondes, transparent nail polish. My slattern was about to be transformed into Cinderella at the ball.

I even agreed to a necklace, a rather pretty plastic thing, blue like her eyes with black pearls, as well as a pair of fake silver and emerald earrings, cheaply made, but they made her smile more than ever.

In the clothing department, I sat down on a stool to wait patiently while she tried on the clothes she had picked out. I wondered why it had no effect on me, all that money vanishing before my eyes. Usually, every euro I spent ripped out some part of myself, of my work, of my ancestors' work, tore away some part of my land. All the hardship, the calluses on my hands, the worry about harvests prevented me from enjoying what I owned, other than through my gaze. But now, on the contrary, I was delighting in it. As I delighted in everything that came from her. I was happy because of her shining eyes, her lips parted on her teeth, her laughter as delicate as a medlar. It was Christmas in July. And I figured I wouldn't be taking my money with me to the cemetery. I could not project myself beyond death, I refused to imagine life without me, the thought terrified me. I knew I was going to have to create a shelter for Suiza, but I didn't know how to go about it, how to protect her enough. I avoided the subject, I fled into the nearest reality the moment the future loomed before me. I could not envisage it without an unprecedented inertia, a staggering lethargy.

I felt a great tremor go through me: I had to admit, sitting there on a plastic stool which threatened to collapse under my weight, dying of heat in my leather jacket I hadn't removed, that if I had to choose between the woman and the land, I would choose the woman, that solitude would never again be an option, even in death. I felt gloomy all of a sudden, discovering this dependency. I had fallen asleep needy, I awoke addicted. But Suiza's childish joy reanimated me, I breathed in a line of happiness, and she massaged my anxious little heart with a very tight wool sweater that made her breasts look like apples. Big ones. I could make out her nipples, hard and erect from the texture of the wool, pointing beneath the slightly stretched fabric. A cliché, but perfectly effective: it gave me a nice steady hard-on and I reflected that I would have to marry her no matter what, so she would be my wife on paper and in the eyes of the world, the priest was right, and then maybe people would stop fighting me over her like dogs over a bone. If I was going to die, I wanted my land to become Suiza's land.

Liar! That was the speech for my private gallery, but I knew very well that in truth, all I wanted was to buy her a little dog collar to wear around her neck: *Property of Tomás López Gabarre, return if found.* A little voice even urged me to have it tattooed on her ass. Or just use a branding iron . . .

She was holding a shirt for me, a fine linen shirt. A new bark for my sun-worn skin. She slipped into my cabin, bigger here, in the men's department, and there was no warder. She took off my old shirt and before putting the new one on me, she put her head on my heart and circled my waist with her white arms. She didn't squeeze, it was just to tell me she was happy, or at least so I supposed. A minute of silence, which resonated inside me like thunder.

I wanted her, but the curtain was too thin, there were people going by and the neon lights were blinding. I picked up the shirt, along with our already numerous purchases, and paid a fortune.

I went outside almost like a thief, looking for a side street, an innocent protective doorway. I interrupted our hurried steps by the oozing stone of an old inner courtyard, dark and humid. She had grasped my intention already a while ago, from the way I kept pulling her toward me; she removed her underpants while I slowly undid a few buttons on my trousers, looking her in the eyes. I took her thighs in my hands and lifted her effortlessly to my height. I pinned her against the wall and, for a few endless seconds, I didn't move, just stared at her, quivering and opalescent on the black stone. I began to move in and out of her, with an excessive, calculated slowness, never taking my eyes off her. She was full of me, breathless, lost. She threw her head back slightly, her eyes clouded over like a pond after a storm, her breasts pointed arrogantly beneath the light fabric. I put my lips on her white neck and nibbled, where her veins were throbbing, to bring her back to me, to keep her under my yoke. I could have lasted a long time, made her come again, but she begged me in a murmur to fuck her again, because she loved my cock and everything that came from me, and she wanted more, wanted me to fuck her until nightfall, wanted me to come to fill her to give her my sperm as a gift to keep deep inside her. Her smooth accent, the mixture of raw and tender words, the exotic little imperfections in her grammar reached their target, I tried not to listen to her anymore, I looked down. And I saw my cock that was shiny with her, huge, pulsing, sliding in the fire-colored silk between her white thighs that I held firmly in my brown hands, while my mind derailed into a nothingness of ecstasy.

We got home late at night, after the restaurant and a long walk along the city walls, the sky heavy with rainclouds and the clashing lights of the city. We walked like tourists wherever the wind and the smells led us, our peaceful gazes stealing the intimacy from inside people's homes below us. Under no obligation where time was concerned, haphazardly governed by our senses, drawn to light like mosquitoes.

She dozed in the car, almost rolled up in a ball in her seat, weary from the noise, exhausted by the fullness of her day. I looked at her now and again. I was proud of her, and it made me proud of me. I smiled to myself in the dark night, wondering how much longer I would go on thinking ironically about earlier, bitter returns, about Ramón and Nacera.

I went to see the priest and the mayor. The wedding would be held after Christmas, because of the paperwork, and the radiotherapy. I was hoping I could hold out until then.

I had come home early because we were gradually slipping toward winter. I went to sit on the bench outside the house, now, I took the time to live. She had fashioned a sort of sun shade with a thick canvas for the days when the sun still flooded the façade. But now most of the time the weather was gloomy, dark and heavy, with sudden, daily downpours. The sky was charged with heavy flat-bottomed clouds of anthracite gray, which curled around their peaks in layers of grayish scrolls. Those days, the earth seemed even more fertile, a lovely warm, velvety brown, nature's chocolate. Green had also joined the party, thick and gleaming, covering everything and preparing to do battle. It got out its entire range, from pale green to emerald, olive, and forest, it reigned as absolute master, seeping onto houses, roads, and sky. If it began to rain, that was its ultimate victory, the rain polished it, drop by drop, leaf by leaf, blade by blade, until the next break in the clouds, when it would shine with a thousand dazzling rays of greenery.

That evening it wasn't raining and I had been able to stay outside for a while. I felt dead tired, vaguely nauseous, but oddly, for the last few days, I had not been coughing as much. I had bought patches, I would stick one on my ass when I remembered to, and now I was only smoking half a pack. On a wobbly old table she had found in the attic, she had set out olives and wine. She had come to sit close to me and we had been speaking for a while already. I was telling her about the land, with simple words, about harvests and what I wanted to do. She told me about the capons, she didn't want to force-feed them anymore because of their sad eyes, and about Josefina's irises, which she had planted at the entrance, now that Ramón had trimmed the fig tree, and about all the space behind the barns where she wanted to make a new orchard together with "My Prince," now that it was all tidy. Apple trees above all, for pies and clafoutis. The little wall, too, that was collapsing at the end of the path. I didn't say much, in the end, she was the one who was chirping away, coming out with plans, suggesting solutions. King Tomás was listening to his Scheherazade, she had more than a thousand and one things to do, and I figured I would not have enough of the little life remaining to accomplish the twenty-four labors of Suiza.

That day, it was a bit different.

"Do you want to be my wife?" I asked straight up.

"I am your wife, you always say."

"Yes, but for the others."

"Everyone knows I am your wife."

"I mean on paper, for the land. So that everything will be yours if something happened to me, if I died."

"If you died, I would die, too."

"Because it's what I would like, what I want."

"If you want, I want."

She waited a little and then she said:

"Could you ask another day?"

"Another day?"

"Yes, ask another day when I forget and ask again with Mass."

"Mass?"

"Mass, big speech. Not like you're asking for bread or meat, or to eat, or for work. You know, like in the movies, where the man he asks with lots of nice words which makes music of I love you and the girl she cries because it's too much happiness for her, she didn't think he was going to ask this, she thought he was going to talk about his car."

"All right."

I would ask Lope about Mass, I was sure he would come up with the Easter mass for me, I would learn it by heart.

After Christmas, I would put a little necklace on her: *If found return to Tomás López Gabarre.*

It would soon be winter, and oddly enough, I felt I was rising from my ashes. The autumn was mild, the balmy air persisted, the forest did not go to sleep.

It was Ramón who saw her first, he ran flat-out to meet her, he was afraid, as I was, that something bad had happened, for her to be coming along like that, in the rain, she never came to the fields as a rule. I left my furrow, turned around in a flash, and revved the tractor, close on his heels. She quickly reassured us, smiling at me and touching Ramón's arm. She pointed at me and came closer, twisting her ankles in the long, soft, freshly-turned furrows.

I opened the door and slowed the tractor for her to climb up next to me, out of the passing shower.

"I need some money."

She shouted a little, because of the engine noise.

"You can take what you want at the grocery, you know that. Luis knows it too, there's no problem."

"Yes, but it's for something for me, it's not for the house."

"How much?"

On a crumpled scrap of paper where the ham had been wrapped, €3.69 was scrawled. I had to keep from smiling.

"That should be fine. But I should have thought of it before you. I'll get you a box, just for you, and put it on the buffet. I'll put the money from the eggs and the poultry in it. Since you're the one who feeds them and looks after them, that money should be yours. I'll also put some money for the housekeeping in there, since you're the one who always cleans."

I stopped off at Luis's on the way home that evening and bought a box for her that opened with a tiny key, a garish pink box with a Cinderella motif. Inside it I put €40, to start off with. So that she wouldn't feel too indebted, I got a box for myself, too, the same one, but in red, with Batman. Luis's entire stock of boxes. That happy imbecile didn't dare say a thing when I sidled up to the counter with my boxes, but his very expression told me he was that close to making a remark, so I felt obliged to explain:

"What? They're for my nephews."

"You have nephews?"

"Sure. Course I do."

"As an only child?"

"They're my nephews by marriage. Maybe you want to see their ID cards?"

"You'll have to introduce them someday, I'll give them some candy."

He was no fool, the bastard, but it was all in good fun.

"Okay, give me a bag though, all right? I don't want to walk around the village with all this."

Suiza liked her pink box, she wiped it off carefully and set it out on the buffet in plain sight. She had clapped her hands and said the ceremonial *Gracias, señor*. There really were times when she was twelve years old.

"One for you, one for me, and the account with Luis for the house, all right?"

"All right."

I had bought a little notebook, too, and I set about explaining prices to her, to give her a scale of values.

I sat her down at the table, took my time, and gave her a brilliant lesson, worthy of a schoolteacher. I put in a huge effort, trying to keep things simple, precise, and concise. I didn't do too badly, calculations, math, and physics were my strong point, I was proud of myself. She listened religiously, but I don't really know why, I had a nagging doubt about how much she understood. I could see she was trying to be attentive two hundred percent of the time: she even forgot to inhale, motionless in a sort of anxiousness which seemed to ooze from her entire being. In the end, I too became very anxious. To please me, she wanted to understand, that much was palpable.

I finished my lecture with a simple question: how much does it cost, if you add the price of a kilo of cod at two euros to a kilo of salt at one euro?

I couldn't see her face, she was bent over the paper, she was thinking, that was good.

"Well?"

She was crying. Big teardrops fell onto my notebook.

I was fuming, I was sure she could understand.

"Make an effort, it's not really that difficult."

She didn't answer.

"I'm going milking, you have all evening to find the answer."

I left her there, like a kid who is not allowed to leave the table until he's finished his plate of leaf spinach, no cream. I left her there, because I had suddenly felt like slapping her, my anger kept me from feeling any compassion, I was annoyed that she was so impervious to my explanations. All of a sudden, I thought she was supremely stupid.

In the cold air in the barn, amid the familiar ruminating of the cows, I calmed down. The animals looked at me with their placid, vacant gaze, and I could feel the guilt welling up inside me.

What the fuck did I care if she didn't know how to count?

I knew, and that was enough for the two of us. What she knew, for the two of us, was how to make an apple pie, jump for joy, laugh about nothing, talk all the time, fold and iron and put the laundry away neat as a pin, slip perfumed handkerchiefs into my jacket pocket for me to come upon by surprise, her breasts in the cashmere sweater, the palm of her hand on my cheek, her soft rosy sex . . .

All of a sudden, I left the cows and ran back to the house, found her right there where I'd left her, in the same position, the same big teardrops falling on the notebook. I tossed the notebook in the fire, knelt down next to her, and murmured:

"You don't know how to count, and I don't know how to teach you, you don't understand. I don't know how to make apple pie, and you couldn't teach me, I wouldn't understand a thing. We'll leave it like that. We'll share: I'll do the counting, and you'll make the apple pie, all right?"

"Oh, yes! It's good like that. You count, I make the apple pie and the food," she said, sniffling loudly.

Unanswerable. I was beginning to understand, too.

She blew her nose noisily in a little handkerchief with birds on it.

"You're not angry, then? I'll make the pie this evening, if you want."

The next day, she was outside Luis's at opening time, I saw her on my way to buy cigarettes at Álvaro's: she was leaning up against the shop window, trying to see inside. She didn't even notice the Seat.

Of course, the grocery was closed: Luis was at the bar, sipping his white wine and lemonade.

"Luis! My wife is waiting for you outside your shop, maybe you could get around to opening for her before she puts down roots."

"I don't goddamn believe it! I can't even finish my coffee in peace! Get a load of this, Álvaro! My wealthy clients are coming to harass me at the crack of dawn!"

"That's a funny-looking coffee you've got there. And as for what you call dawn: it's already half past ten."

Luis had been breakfasting on white wine since nine o'clock, clinging to the slot machine.

"She just wants to buy something that costs €.69."

He croaked something again about wasn't that just typical dumb women, wanting to disturb everyone for no reason at all, that she'd already been there yesterday driving him up the wall about some little magazine, wanting to write down the price, and look at it every which way, and leaving the shop and coming back to look at it again. He topped it all off with, "For a piece of crap like that."

I passed Suiza on my way back, she was carrying the "piece of crap" as if it were a newborn baby, and she remained oblivious when I sounded the horn, completely absorbed in her little burden.

That evening when I got home, I switched on the light, anxious. As a rule, when I came in everything was ready, and the house lit up the entire countryside.

"Is everything all right?"

"Yes."

She hesitated, still surprised.

"What time it is?"

Not waiting for my reply, she sprang to her feet. She suddenly remembered who I was.

"We're going to eat."

"What were you doing?"

"Painting!"

She almost shouted, relieved, the brush still in her hand, a big smile on her face, happy to show me what she had done. I looked at it. It was a hen. I knew that hen. It was not a real hen like on a photograph, nor did the technique have the perfection of a Zurbarán, it was a hen of extreme, living simplicity, the way you picture a hen when you think of one. As a rule, painting did nothing for me. But that hen, there, I had to acknowledge that it was a good hen, ready to squawk.

"I don't have the right brush, I need smaller," she said, as if to apologize, given my silence.

"I like it. It's pretty. Where did you find the paint?"

"At Luis's."

She shoved a kid's magazine in my face, *Learn to Paint with Disney*, which offered as a present, with its first issue, a little box of basic, faded watercolors, and a shitty brush that had at best two bristles to it. Wild boar bristles, maybe.

On Saturday, it was raining so hard there was even too much water for plowing. Once I'd picked Suiza up at Francesa's, I carried on to Lugo, on impulse, because I wanted to buy her some paint. Lope had taught me this: when I gave her a present, it was as if I were giving myself something, so I didn't hesitate anymore. I took her to a specialized bookseller's and stationer's. They had gouache in jars and tubes and pots, of every kind and color. Upon the advice of the salesman, because it was a good thick paint, and she wouldn't be disappointed, she chose a big box of tubes of acrylic, with basic colors. I asked her to pick out some colors that were out of the ordinary. She took only green tones. It's true that in Galicia, that was all you needed. I wanted to buy her canvases, too, but she categorically refused, she preferred wood. But she did get some good brushes, fine, medium, one very large. The salesman suggested some wood varnish to make the paintings shiny, once they were finished. She said yes, she explained that she wanted her rain to sparkle in the sun, like in reality.

When we got back, I didn't take the time to eat, I cut pieces of wood of every size, an entire supply of supports for her painting. I knew she would be capable of trying to cut them herself if I didn't do it, and I preferred her with fingers.

"Will you do a painting for me?" I asked, to make her happy.

"Whatever you want."

"I'd like the house with the forest behind it."

She gratified me with a caress on the cheek, an angelic smile, and perhaps it was these little, attentive gestures that made me happiest.

She had absolutely no notion of monetary value, and sometimes murmured a word to indicate she would like a simple slice of ewe's cheese, say, or some *chipirones*, which she was particularly fond of. I knew she wasn't with me for my money, my fortune was way beyond anything she could imagine.

She began painting every day and time no longer had any definite hold on her. She had set up in a room downstairs, one of the ones we didn't use. I had cut up a big board and fashioned two trestles to make her a sort of rustic workbench. She had placed it under the window for more light. She preferred painting on the flat, otherwise her arm begin to ache. She could go and paint for an hour and didn't have to put everything away afterwards. I had given her a little alarm clock I never used, so she wouldn't miss mealtimes, because when she began painting, she did not see the time go by. She asked me to set it for "one hour before you come back," so she'd have time to set the table and prepare everything. I had assured her that I didn't mind, I was willing to be patient and eat later, to wait for her to finish, but she said, putting it rather nicely:

"Painting mustn't eat real life."

One evening, she came to get me in my workshop.

"I finished your painting, I'll show you, if you want. You won't laugh?"

"No."

I studied it. It was huge. She had used the biggest panel of wood.

There was the sky, the forest, the house, and two people in the foreground. The two of us, obviously. It showed both great finesse and a certain naïveté. What I liked was the way she had done the sky, it made the forest so beautiful, a sky before rain; she was like a photographer who knows his model's best angle. The forest appeared to be one huge mass, which was true to reality, but when I went closer, I could see she had painted tiny leaves one by one, with different colors, depending on whether they were young or old. She knew the trees by heart, like I did. It was the same for the house. She knew the house's drowsiness, as it nestled against the edge of the forest. She had understood everything, decrypted everything, translated everything, she read my land better than I could myself. She might never be able to count, but she knew how to read my nature and painted it better than anyone. I was tall and dark, almost as big as the house, and Suiza was tiny and all white. I was holding her by the hand and I had a fire of bright red flames in my lungs.

Now, for once, I might have been moved by a painting, but it was surely because she had done it. I hung it ceremoniously on the wall, it was gigantic. When she varnished it, the colors became deeper, and they shone. At noon, I stood for a long time gazing at the painting, drinking my glass of wine. I didn't really know if it was beautiful—what did I know about art—I just felt that it told the story of my life. No need to go up to the attic anymore, I had brought the guitar down.

As for Ramón, he was sure it was beautiful.

"It's beautiful, I tell you. Yeah! It's beautiful!" He was ecstatic, his eyes half-closed in the smoke of his cigarette. "The forest more than anything. Fuck, is that good, that forest, it looks like it's going to move. And the house! It's really good, huh, don't you think? The house is really like that. The stones, it looks like she's counted them. The fence . . . maybe you should give it a fresh coat of paint, your fence. And you, Tomás? That's really you, isn't it! Dark as an Arab, big as a grouper. That's really you. With your burned lungs."

Then, turning around all at once, as if a revelation had struck him, he said, "Do you think she'd do one for me?"

"Ask her."

Lope had helped me with the milking, I was feeling super woozy again. The oncologist said that everything was looking fine for the moment, but I got impression he was taking me for ride.

"Boss, I have to tell you something. Your wife came to see me yesterday, to buy a thing at Luis's, a gnome."

"A gnome? What the fuck?"

"You know, those little characters out of legends. Where I'm from in Asturias, there are loads of them. My favorite one is the Trasgou."

"How old are you, anyway?"

"It's not a question of age, boss, it's a question of belief. My grandmother used to tell me stories about the gnomes in the woods or in people's houses. I liked them. I believe a little. They're like guardian angels, more or less."

"So you're telling me that Luis has guardian angel gnomes . . . What are you taking at the moment? Is it legal, whatever you're smoking?"

"Yes, he's got them, boss, little plaster statues, things for tourists. They're not cheap, but you can probably still bargain with him, he's not selling the things, there are no tourists around here. And besides, they've been in his window so long they're all dusty and faded. But your woman, she believes in them, they must have the same thing where she's from. There's one she wants that's twelve euros, she came to ask me if that's expensive."

After milking, I headed over to see Luis.

"Sell me all your gnomes, will you?"

"My gnomes?"

I went out to show him the little statues stuck between the shop window and an indescribable jumble.

"Oh yeah, those things. Are they for your nephews by marriage?"

"Precisely! How much for one?"

"Twelve euros."

"You've gotta be kidding!"

"No, I swear, they come from I don't know where, they're hand-painted, by little orphans who—"

"Spare me the saga for tenderhearted old ladies. I'll buy all of them, I'll take them off your hands. Make me a price. How many have you got?"

"Well . . . there are three here, and I must have two left at the back of the store."

"So five. Your price?"

"Five euros apiece?"

It was a question, he was afraid I'd clout him.

"Sold!"

"I'll wrap them in newspaper for you so they won't break."

"Can you put some gift wrap, too?"

"I don't have any more. But if you want, I have a nice box for €1.50."

"You're a good salesman, Luis. Sell me your shitty box with the rest."

"It's not a shitty box, look: your wife will love it, it's a Hello Kitty box, girls love it."

"Who says it's for my wife?"

"I don't know how many times she's asked me the price of those statues and yesterday I wrote 'twelve euros' on the wrapping for the ham. I can just tell . . . You see what I mean. I just know that she'll like the box, she asked the price for it, too, twice already. What can I say, girls and pink are a sure hit."

"Did she ask about the price for anything else?"

"No, for the time being that's it. But if you'd like to make her happy, you could add some roasted corn nuts. And a few candies, especially these soft things, they taste like strawberry. She often comes to buy them, but she only takes a few and pays for them separately, and she stands eating them by the window, not to take them home, she must think you wouldn't like it."

"Oh? Give me a kilo, then."

"A kilo?!"

"A kilo in another box."

"I don't have any more Hello Kitty boxes, but I have SpongeBob SquarePants."

"Go for SpongeBob SquarePants."

"About the gnomes, you don't mind if I tell them at the bar that I sold them to some Americans? Everyone's been teasing me about them for God knows how long."

"No problem. Tell the Pope, if you want."

"I have to tell you something, Tomás. I do like your wife. And not just because I know that when she comes, she'll ensure me of the day's turnover. She's kind. Just the way she says thank you all the time, whenever I put something on the counter. People around here they come in, barely say hello, and give their order. Sort of the way you do, if you don't mind my saying so. She always asks how I'm doing, and I swear, she waits for my answer."

"I know she's kind."

"And then there's the way things always surprise her, even insignificant things. You should have seen her face when I gave her the Dijon mustard I ordered especially for her! I swear, it was as if I had found her the Holy Grail of O Cebreiro. When she leaves I always wonder if they're all like that, the Swiss, or if it's just that we've forgotten our manners—kindness, tenderness, even joy. After that, the old people seem older, the women seem grouchier, and the men seem harder."

"We're the ones who've forgotten, Luis. But we can remember and learn again. I promise I'll ask you how you are next time. And I'll try to wait for your answer."

She made a painting for Ramón. He didn't really know what he wanted, so she suggested a portrait, just to see. He sat for her several afternoons in a row. He was posing, trying to look the charmer, the hero. With his chin raised, his hank of hair combed and shiny under his hat, his slightly protuberant lips on the verge of a fictitious kiss, sometimes he would wink. One arm outstretched, his strong, gnarly hand on the handle of his umbrella. Inscrutable and focused, Suiza painted, ignoring his mimes, and sometimes I would come to enjoy the silence of the session, a beer in my hand, it was entertaining to see the pair of them playing their roles to perfection, the painter and her model. He wanted her to represent him from head to toe, standing in front of a little pedestal table where a magnificent octopus lay inside a huge soup tureen he had inherited from his mother, and with a luminescent Holy Virgin of Fátima he had brought back from a pilgrimage in his youth. She was painting on a long board cut from a tree, almost as tall as he was.

It wasn't a photograph, it wasn't perfect, but as always, it was strikingly true. Bit by bit I could see Ramón coming to life. The old man, just as I imagined him when I thought about him. It was really him, with his cigarettes, his lovely velvet brown eyes, his big crumpled black hat, and the fine white wrinkles that streaked his skin, weathered by sun and wind. He was standing, thin in his big raincoat the color of sodden earth, leaning proudly on the black umbrella with its sculpted wooden handle, which never left him.

Once it was varnished, his gaze came alive.

He beamed with joy.

"I'll hang it in my bedroom. It will have its own spot. Old Edelmira, my landlady, will be jealous as a magpie."

He hugged Suiza as if he were wringing her out or saying goodbye forever, and then he painstakingly wrapped his painting in an old blanket, once he'd asked twenty times over whether the paint was really dry. He carried his treasure to the bar to show everyone and puff himself up with importance. I followed him, allegedly to help him carry the magnum opus; I was simply too eager not to miss anything.

It became the event of the day, the art and letters review. Everyone analyzed the technique, the colors, the pose. Everyone agreed on the fact that the octopus was so realistic it looked like it was about to slide out of the soup tureen, and that Ramón was about to speak, and the Virgin was about to appear. We drank to his health, raised our glasses to the painting, it was his entry into the Pantheon, a eulogy. Blissful, crimson with pride, drunk as a skunk, Ramón proclaimed to anyone who would listen that he would end up in the Prado, next to *Las Meninas* or *El tres de mayo*.

I didn't say anything, but as God is my witness I was as proud as a peacock, all that was missing was a fan on my ass.

One misty morning, I asked Lope:

"Do you believe in God, Lope?"

"Why are you asking me that, boss? You think you're going to die?"

"No, just asking."

"It depends if I need to. I don't really think of it that way. I only ask myself why I need to believe. And you, boss?"

"Oh, well . . . "

I didn't dare tell him that, in the state I was in, I would have believed any crank who brainwashed me with a multitude of psalms and followed him to the ends of the earth, wearing hip-pie sandals and a long white toga, to end up committing sui-cide along with all my shaven-headed buddies, emaciated from months of fasting and macrobiotic food. All of a sudden, it did me a world of good to think that everything that was happening to me was down to the goodwill of a supreme, almighty being who had the power of life or death over my insignificant person. Perhaps all I had to do then was make him happy, rub his back, change my ways and self-flagellate for him to graze me with a magic finger that would cure me there on the spot. Illness was making me extraordinarily naive, borderline imbecilic.

I didn't dare tell anyone about what was preoccupying me, least of all the priest. Through all my reading, education, and studies, I had acquired a very poor opinion of religion. For me, it was nothing but obscurantism, inquisition, a ferment of frat-ricidal wars, self-alienation, and the oppression of the unedu-cated working masses, particularly in Spain. My repudiation had developed very early on, when I used to attend mass as an adolescent because my father obliged me to go there in his place. I was so extremely bored that I had to struggle between falling asleep and the hilarious laughter caused by a senile old priest who paraphrased the Bible, although I didn't really know what he was talking about. I would wait impatiently for the only moment I liked, communion, which for a few seconds would calm the ferocious rumbling of my stomach, for I had invariably set out without breakfast, and as I walked down the aisle to go back to my seat I would play at looking as inspired as possible. Now, as I was sick and trying to team up with God, I felt as if I were rejecting the ideas of my youth, losing some of my intelligence and discernment; in short, I was turn-ing into a churchy old man. I did not speak of my sudden new faith to anyone for I was filled with shame, and afraid some-one would make fun of my abrupt reconversion into the resident fundamentalist Catholic. This sense of shame astonished me, as well. In the village, everyone went around baying their faith, displaying it ostentatiously. I found myself hugging the walls and thinking with the outer extremities of a few neurons: I believe that I might just possibly believe. I had been stunned, too, when in the space of two card games, I had managed to tell Javier, the council employee, that I suspected I believed in God. He wouldn't shut up after that, the fatso, firm believer that he was. Since he thought I was on his side, he launched into a laudatory speech about God, the angels, and all the holy patrimony. Singularly, his speech, instead of reassuring me regarding the well-founded nature of my new aspirations, merely filled me with a terrible doubt.

She painted a picture for Francesa, a big surprise to thank her for the lessons. The old woman had a book about Paris and Suiza had asked her if she could borrow it, supposedly to show it to me.

In fact, it was so she could copy the "Place du Tertre," since that was where Francesa used to go with Carlos to eat ice cream on Sundays and days off in the spring. She wanted to give her "a little bit of France in all this Spain, like a little bit of butter in all the olive oil." She had a lot of difficulty with the painting, but she was pleased with the result. It was exactly like the square in the book, made in Suiza, with a spring breeze causing everything to rustle, and two figures seen from behind, tenderly kissing.

When Suiza gave her the painting, Francesa wept like a fountain in the worst of the summer heat: not much water but a great deal of sniffling, and she refused the milk and the eggs, saying she didn't want to be paid anymore, since she was in far greater need of Suiza than her student was of Spanish lessons. She said that the pupil now spoke as well as her teacher, even better, and it was a disgrace if anyone had ever thought she was stupid. I had to get angry, invoke my honor as a Spaniard, and my word, and strike my breast with my fist, for her to accept what I had brought her. And then I abruptly asked her if she would agree to be Suiza's witness at the wedding, and she began to weep even harder. I bit my lip and realized I should have waited for another day. The painting and the wedding, that was too much for one visit.

* * *

I put all the gnomes on the windowsill in the bedroom, once I had washed them and touched them up with a little paint. I kissed them, we love each other, the gnomes and me. They protect me. I leave the window open so they can go back in the forest at night when they want. The one who has another gnome on his back, his name is one, and the other one with the big smile and the round belly, his name is two. "My Prince" told me that when they go off at night into the woods, and they're not here anymore, it's zero. If you put the one next to the other, the two, and they hold hands, that makes twelve. If there is one who goes off without the other, that makes ten or twenty. Both of them have a penetrating gaze. "My Prince" also said that one is really one and a half, since he has a baby gnome on his back. I understood. Now I know a little about numbers. I mustn't tell Tomasse, because he doesn't know anything about pies.

* * *

Suiza painted a portrait of Euserbio for Josefina, slightly in profile, standing next to his mother with his arm around her. With the church in the background. It was easy for her to paint Euserbio because Josefina always shows her the same ID photo, perfectly preserved in its plastic sleeve, a photo she worships like a relic. In my opinion, she knows him mainly because she has heard so much about him, as if she had read him in braille.

She invited Josefina to come and drink coffee at six in the afternoon. I came back for the cake, a specialty from her country, a clafoutis with apples, which I liked at least as much as the pie. No sooner had Josefina sat down than Suiza gave her the present, eager to see her reaction. The old lady opened the package, took the painting, and remained very silent. I was tense and worried, even more so than Suiza, my mouth open, waiting for Josefina's opinion, I was afraid she might say it was crap. Suddenly she stood up and declared solemnly, her eyes riveted on the painting:

"My girl, I will say thank you tomorrow, that's enough emotion for today. I am just going to go home with my Euserbio, I think he has something to tell me."

She left us there like two nitwits, I ate the cake all by myself, but it was smaller than usual.

That left only Lope. He didn't know what he wanted. He had no idea. I told Suiza about Luis Caballero, I'd seen a few of his paintings in Madrid. Back then I had thought they were shocking: naked men's bodies, full of tension, in unequivocal positions, but I was older now and I realized that what had shocked me above all was the excitement I felt on seeing male members. I was afraid of liking it.

She came up with the idea of painting two young peasants at harvest time. One was lying on his side, bare chested, his back turned, listening to the other, who was facing him, leaning on a haystack, in a light, white shirt open on his hairless, slightly muscular chest. I don't know how she did it, or why, but they gave off a torrid eroticism I found disturbing. The scene was meant to be bucolic and lighthearted, but it evoked something else: the force of desire, of lust, of sex. Beneath its casual veneer of romanticism, the painting reeked of sex.

Lope smiled, imperceptibly. He turned to Suiza:

"Madame, it is marvelous!" he said in French.

Ramón gulped.

"Look, I don't know, but if I were you, I wouldn't take that one to the bar."

We all agreed.

The following week, I started on Suiza's paperwork.

If I wanted to marry her, I had to establish her identity. I made the most of a trip "My Prince" took to Madrid to ask him to start the procedure with the consulate. Suiza had no ID papers—she had lost everything on her way here. We had to start from scratch.

One day when they were speaking in private, she had told Lope she wasn't Swiss, but French. That great lover of France came rushing up to me to let me know, pleased as punch, because now he could understand why he felt such a particular tenderness for her: he'd always had an intuitive affinity with French women.

"How do you know, where do you usually see them, these French women?"

He paused to think for a moment, and I burst out laughing, pleased with my snide remark. I didn't want him to be better acquainted with French women than I was.

He came back that afternoon to put me in my place:

"I see them in novels, boss, French women. They're always the same, passionate, overcome by their emotions. And when it comes to novels, I'm sure I've read more than you have."

To the people in the village, she went on being Swiss. They were used to having it that way, and they already had a French woman, Francesa. We didn't let the cat out of the bag.

There was the fact, too, that just before Christmas, Ramón had ordered a "Made in Switzerland" calendar for Suiza from

Luis, because he wanted to give her a present that would remind her of her country.

And of course, when he got it, he went to show it off at the café and all around the village: the vineyards of Lavaux in autumn, Geneva and its lake, the Matterhorn in the snow, and so on. He pitched his stories so well that everyone was convinced that before she ended up with us, Suiza had lived in a wooden chalet in the shadow of the Matterhorn and would take the little Gornergrat train every day to Zermatt. There she ate nothing but cheese fondue and chocolate, and in her garden a huge red flag with an immaculate white cross fluttered constantly in the wind. The legend grew, and a few days later, she had become an heiress to the Russian tsars who had found refuge incognito among Swiss high society, then fled to Spain when she was unmasked by President Putin's clever spies. They had pursued her all through Switzerland, France, and Spain. They had caught up with her not far from our village, then sequestered and tortured her for over a week, without her ever confessing a thing. They had eventually gotten rid of her, thinking they had left her for dead in Paula's chicken coop, with her brain fried by electroshock torture.

I let the rumors circulate. It flattered me: I wouldn't be marrying just anybody.

I knew that marriage would change nothing between us, that our days would be the same. But the priest was right, the village men saw her in a better light now that they knew my intentions: marriage amounted to a deed of property, she was no longer some homeless stray, she had a master, cantankerous as he was, and property here had an almost divine value. Now the old men would sigh a respectful *señora* when they passed her in the street, nodding slightly to greet her, and raise their hats. But once she'd walked past them, they would turn around all the same, the way they had always done, to take a good look at her ass.

For the women, it changed nothing. They had already accepted her long ago, I only came to realize this late in the day. Initially I had thought it was simple female solidarity, but it was something else. I put my finger precisely on what I had always perceived unconsciously: women, even when they were socially or emotionally impoverished, were less damaged than men. In spite of deprivation, emptiness, or solitude, they always had a little love to give, as if they were born with a bigger supply. Like Luis, but right from the start, they had been touched by Suiza, by her naïveté, her fresh outlook, and the way she took care to show her gratitude. I understood this one summer day when I went to pick her up at Francesa's. She had come out early, as Francesa had to go to Don Confreixo's to have her prescriptions renewed. Instead of waiting there doing nothing, Suiza had decided to start walking in my direction, taking her time. I saw her on the road, where she had stopped outside Marta's garden to gaze silently and attentively at her climbing beans. Before I reached her, old Marta went out and opened her dry, knotty hand to give her a handful of pods. Fleshy white beans, monstrous in size, in her little emaciated, brittle claw. Suiza had kissed her and all the way home she held her beans in her hand, against her chest. The two women had not exchanged a word, everything had been said through their gaze, their hands. The language of women who have nothing but love. Marta lived below the poverty line, and her only pride in her difficult life was her potatoes and her beans, which she sold at the market on Monday mornings, and which were unlike any others. That was all she had to give, and Suiza received the gift as it was, like a little treasure of love.

"My Prince" had prepared a fine speech for me, full of poetry, with a magnificent conclusion in French which he made me rehearse in the middle of plowing so that I wouldn't stammer at the fateful moment. For the mass and the speech, I was in great shape, all I needed now was the place to utter my vows: I was hesitating between a chic restaurant in Lugo, where the menu cost an arm and a leg and the tablecloths hung down to the floor, or two days in Madrid to go and sign the papers and walk along the Gran Vía. There, too, "My Prince" set me on the right path: best to rely on simple, solid values. He knew a good seafood restaurant in Tapia de Casariego, where you could have the best *chipirones* on the planet, caught that morning, as you sat by a picture window that protected you from the mist and overlooked the ocean and the port. He suggested I rent a little boat and make my declaration out at sea, but to be careful to check the forecast first, and do it one day when the weather was as fine as possible, the sea calm and smooth and as blue as her eyes. I thanked him for his suggestion, telling him that yes, he most definitely had an intuitive affinity with Frenchwomen, and he knew women much better than I did. He went bright pink with emotion.

That morning, it wasn't quite springtime yet, but there was something in the wind that felt like life. The birds at sunrise called out the news. It was their deafening concert at the edge of the eucalyptus trees that woke us up at dawn, long before milking.

Lope and Ramón were at the ready after coffee, we chopped some wood. I had bought a new tractor, it was red, they fought over who would get to drive it, but I was boss. They had to be reminded, somehow. For a while now, those two had been ganging up on me to obtain prerogatives that were far above their condition as farmhands, and I only resisted listlessly. I felt myself letting go there too.

Suiza had not been feeling well for a few days. She looked paler than usual, if that was even possible. Almost transparent. I even wondered for a few seconds whether cancer was contagious.

I'd had a backache for a week, and even on the new tractor with its comfortable seat, I felt these shooting pains. Sometimes, I had to climb down so I could stand straighter and ease the pain. Then I would suggest that Ramón or Lope take up the torch, and they were both as happy as kids. They would have finished me off with a few whacks of the shovel just to get up there in my place.

"Guys, I'm going home for a bit, I have a backache, I must have pulled a muscle, I'll go take an aspirin."

"Maybe you should go back to see Don Confreixo, kid,

forgive me for telling you straight out, but you look terrible today."

"I'll do that. In any case, I have to go see him for the results of yesterday's scan. You and Lope finish up. If you want, I'll ask Alberto to come and replace me."

"It will be all right, boss, with the young man here we'll manage fine. Don't worry. Go get some rest."

He'd been looking at me for a while with palpable fear on his face, cringing a little as he spoke to me, and turning his head to one side as if I were about to explode and he was afraid of getting body parts in his face. It was pretty frightening, I wondered if he wasn't right to be wary. I let them quarrel over who would start first, and I climbed into the Seat as gingerly as possible, because the sagging old seat was real torture.

Don Confreixo called me on the way back, he wanted to see me right away, about the results.

He fit me in between two appointments, as soon as I arrived. From his face alone, I knew I was fucked.

Metastases on C7 and D1, along with cuter little ones on the adrenal glands. The oncologist was suggesting some local radiotherapy to relieve the pain and a high dose of chemotherapy so I would die quicker.

I looked Don Confreixo straight in the eye and said no. No to everything, to the treatments, to going back and forth to the hospital, to medical appointments. I just wanted not to suffer and I had an idea about how to go about it.

I walked home, I needed some fresh air. My only problem was Suiza. I could no longer duck the issue, I had to find a solution.

I threw up again this morning. I'm pregnant. I may be stupid but I know that much. I'm thinking about the baby. Oh! When I think about it, it makes two Suizas in me. The first one laughs, she's happy. Not that sort of great joy you're going to shout from every rooftop because it's so powerful, just a little music buzzing in your head, quietly. I'm happy, tralala, I'm happy. You smile all the time, you think that suddenly your life is like the cottony feeling from when you've had a glass of sweet white wine, out in the sunshine, before you've had anything to eat. But then there is the second Suiza, the one who's afraid. The big nasty fear that overcomes you all of a sudden, makes you want to wet your pants, or run away as fast as you can, with the hair on your neck standing on end and shivers all down your spine.

This fear that they'll come and take my baby. I remember what the girls in the home used to say, especially the ones in the room above, Priscilla and Morgane, "Girls like us aren't allowed to have babies, even if they want. If you know you're pregnant, wait until you feel it moving before you tell anyone, because then you can be sure they won't mess with your head anymore and take you to the hospital so you'll let them remove it since you wouldn't know how to manage, since you have no money and no family, no 'intermediary.'" "What do you mean by intermediary?" I would ask. "I don't know, but you haven't got one, so trust me.

"And besides, you can't stay here, there's nothing here for

babies. *If they can't remove it from your belly right away because it's already too big, they send you to another home in Besançon. It doesn't say prison on the door but it's as good as. And to get in there you have to have a 'something-or-other' plan, too. But don't worry about the plan, the social worker will tell you what to say, she has all the right answers. Above all, you have to say you are really committed to your pregnancy.*" "*What do you mean by committed?*" "*I don't know, but something like you'll know how to manage. Right away you figure out what to call it, and you buy some clothes, that's what the social workers like. And you let the midwife come, too. The midwife is nice, she always wants you to keep the baby, she's never afraid you won't manage. You just tell her you've stopped smoking, and you don't drink beer anymore, and you want to learn what to do to give birth: that's what she really likes to hear. Well, the lessons they give you are nothing but crap, you go with a bunch of women who just talk about their problems and tell you their life story and at the end you do these weird things to relax so you can 'stand the pain of the contractions,' but it doesn't work, Vanessa said that when you're giving birth you still feel like you've got a baobab up your ass.*

"*Once the baby is born, they try again to take it away from you but it's harder, you have to have really done some incredibly stupid things for them to take it, like forgetting the baby and going out to party at nightclubs because you've had enough of changing diapers. There are things you can say to show you're a good mother, the way they want. You can ask Coralie, she copied them down in a notebook to learn them by heart. But don't forget: if you're pregnant, don't tell them, or really only if you can't do otherwise . . .*"

My baby is moving a lot, I can tell them, they won't take it from me, and Tomasse won't let them, I'm sure of that. He keeps everything, even me. I'll have to go see the doctor during my painting time with the money from my Cinderella box. I can go *to the doctor alone now, I don't need to be accompanied. This thing is, you have to make an appointment, and I don't know how to do that. Should I ask "My Prince?" No I can't, babies are a girl thing. Okay, never mind, I'll just go there, I'll stay in the waiting room, and we'll see.*

He's a nice man, Don Confreixo, he guessed right away. Because the baby was already big, he said. I had to have a blood test, and an ultrasound, and go back there three more times before I would go and give birth at the hospital in Lugo. The baby would be in time for strawberries, a fine springtime baby. I ABSOLUTELY had to tell Tomasse, he would know what to do. I had to tell him ABSOLUTELY, because Tomasse needed this, at this time, he wasn't in very good shape, he had to take a lot of medicine and didn't want to. Maybe with the strawberry baby he would take it, now. Don Confreixo seemed really happy for Tomasse.

I had to ask my question. I waited until I was almost out the door, and I figured if he said yes, I would run away:

"They won't take the baby away from me because I don't know what to do?"

He looked at me with those eyes Papa used to have when he said, "What stupid things you say sometimes, my poor girl, whatever gave you such an idea, is it your mother who put these notions in your head?" But right away after, it was Maman's eyes, "No, my little chick, don't worry, I'm sure you'll manage, you just have to make a little effort." The doctor smiled, with his real words he said that if we had to have diplomas to raise children, animals wouldn't have any at all, and that in the end, if you looked a little closer, they were doing a lot better job than us humans were. "Trust me," he added, "I know you will be a good mother, and Tomasse will help you. Try to tell him as soon as you can. Tell him without delay."

When I went out it was raining. Really hard. All around my umbrella it was Niagara Falls. I wanted to walk without the umbrella, to feel the water washing my face, but I was afraid the baby might get cold. I just tilted it to one side so the drops could kiss me. Just three minutes, I knew three, three was the gnome for love. I asked out loud:

"Do you like the rain, baby?"

Of course, you nincompoop! It was a baby from Galicia, it already liked rain and the sea.

My problem was how to tell Tomasse. I had to make it into a pretty poem, or the end of a movie, something like that. In Cindy's American series, there was a girl, Kimberley, who came running into the room like a tornado and murmured to Brandon, "I have to tell you, I went to the gynecologist today, I am carrying your child, it is the most beautiful day of my life." Brandon went all mushy, he took her in his arms and you could see that for him, too, it was the most beautiful day of his life. I had to find something bigger than, "My love, it's magnificent, you're going to be a father." Granny Yvette's bun in the oven? I didn't know, I don't know how to talk about important things.

When I got home, I found the answer. Painting. He understood me better with my painting, and I knew how to say things better, without necessarily having to explain.

For two days I'd been stewing, wondering what to do, how to solve the problem. I would roll myself a little cigarette and lean back in my chair, giving in to the great weariness. I hadn't finished the cutting, I was running late because that fucking new tractor broke down for an entire day. I didn't give a damn about anything, I knew I wouldn't even see the springtime, the first seeds coming up. Ramón and Lope went on without me with the old tractors.

I looked up at the painting from force of habit. I saw something had changed: I saw the baby.

I put the tobacco and the papers back down on the table, I slowly stood up and approached from the right, leaning slightly to the left. A black, anxious crab, almost a scorpion. I didn't dare confront it face on, I wanted to be mistaken. But there it was, in Suiza's arms. With its father's skin and its mother's eyes. It looked peaceful and serene, a smile full of trust lighting up its face. It was a child that had just been born, the baby that came to my mind when as an adolescent I dreamt of babies. The perfect mixture of darkness and light, strength and frailty.

And I began crying like an idiot.

This huge mass of meat, of flesh and blood, this big thick brute began sobbing like a kid, quietly at first, then louder, huge sobs. I was weeping like a little boy, and thinking strange things, about the sadness of not having it in my belly, that baby, about my father and my mother, who would never see it either, and all the men like me, and my death foretold, just when at last I could have been happy.

She didn't leave me alone for very long. She came close to me to hear the storm raging in my chest. Her warmth calmed me for a moment, I was no longer alone in the torment of my feelings. She must have thought I was happy, that I was weeping for joy, and I could not confess to her that it was with rage. I took her face between my hands, smeared it with my tears, and murmured, squeezing very hard:

"My love. I love you."

I had to play the perfect father, put on an act, make it seem as if all the trumpets in Jericho had begun sounding the good news. I could not spoil the party, not now. I had to let her have a little time still. I held her, I was afraid they would take her from me already and mistreat her. I said the typical stupid things:

"I don't want you going to look after the turkeys anymore, they're too aggressive, they might hurt you. And I don't want you carrying the shopping from Luis's, it's too heavy for the baby, you can leave it there, and I'll go get it in the evening. No more riding the bicycle either, you might fall. And you have to take naps, now, for sure, and get your rest. I'll go and see Don Confreixo and find out what we have to do. Is there anything you want? You should eat more at lunch, with orange juice, and drink less coffee."

I was speaking too quickly, I wasn't sure she understood everything, but it was fairly realistic. I said tender things, even though my heart was pierced with terror. I knew confusedly that I was going to have find a better way to protect her, and that it wouldn't be possible. The child was going to be born, and I was going to die.

I went around in circles all afternoon. I knew that all this just wasn't possible. The little baby, with its father dead, and its mother incapable. Around me there were only old people. No one I could trust to leave the two of them with, and to run the farm, and take care of the bank accounts. I watched her working, happy and busy, as if nothing had changed. She was buzzing away as she scrubbed the windowpanes. I wanted to say to her: don't mess with that, come on, let's go to the seaside, but pain and fatigue left me drained and nauseous on my chair. What could I do?

That evening, I brought my father's rifle down from the attic. I said I had some bookkeeping to do, so she would go ahead to bed on her own, and I held her for a long time on my lap, to touch her, caress her one last time. I didn't overdo it either, she mustn't suspect anything, there were times she had a sixth sense that made her clairvoyant. She knew how to read me, she knew when I was anxious, perhaps because of that distance I would create between us without actually realizing. Often, when she was worried, she would come up to me and say, "Do you still love me?" And that was when I knew I wasn't well. This time, she didn't say anything, I had been sufficiently taciturn and affectionate for her to go into the room and lie down after a last kiss.

I smoked a final cigarette in the pure Galician night. The silent forest enfolded me into its fragrance. The silence was thick, like before a storm, although the sky was clear. I knew the turbulence was inside me, and that the rumbling could be heard in my heart alone. With less in the way of lungs, my heart had more room, it could pound away, resonate. There was an echo.

For the livestock, I had asked Lope to replace me at milking the next morning, I knew he was the one who would get there first, he was more solid than the old man.

In the space of a few minutes, in my death wish, I had programmed everything down to the last detail. I would walk quietly to the bedroom, look at her one last time. She would be sleeping on her side, serenely, her lips slightly parted as usual.

She would offer me her temple, all I had to do was pull the trigger. I would hesitate for a few seconds. Not long. I would fire. With the detonation, she would move a bit, as if to get up, then fall back against the pillow. There would be a little hole where I fired, it would be clean. I didn't doubt that underneath it would be gorier, and I mustn't look. Mustn't touch her anymore. She would remain beautiful, her big blue eyes open. She wouldn't have time to notice that she was dead. The child, too, would be surprised, not to hear anything anymore, not to receive anything, suddenly, but its death would be slower and gentler. It would gradually drift off.

I would feel no remorse, just infinite sadness.

And then I would put the barrel in my mouth, and where I was concerned, I would not hesitate for a single second.

ABOUT THE AUTHOR

Bénédicte Belpois lives in Besançon, where she works as a midwife. She spent her childhood in Algeria. *Suiza*, her first novel, was written during a long stay in Galicia.